Hear the Dead Cry

Hear the Dead Cry
CHARLIE PRICE

CORGI BOOKS

HEAR THE DEAD CRY
A CORGI BOOK 978 0 552 57323 8

First published under the title, DEAD CONNECTION in the United States as a
Deborah Brodie Book by Roaring Brook Press in 2006, Roaring Brook Press is a division
of Holtzbrinck Publishing Holdings Limited Partnership

First published in Great Britain by Corgi Books,
an imprint of Random House Children's Books
A Random House Group Company

This edition published 2010

13 5 7 9 10 8 6 4 2

The Random House Group Limited supports The Forest Stewardship
Council® (FSC®), the leading international forest-certification organisation.
Our books carrying the FSC label are printed on FSC®-certified paper.
FSC is the only forest-certification scheme supported by the leading
environmental organisations, including Greenpeace. Our
paper procurement policy can be found at
www.randomhouse.co.uk/environment

MIX
Paper from
responsible sources
FSC
www.fsc.org   FSC® C018072

Corgi Books are published by Random House Children's Books,
61–63 Uxbridge Road, London W5 5SA

www.kidsatrandomhouse.co.uk
www.rbooks.co.uk

Addresses for companies within The Random House Group Limited
can be found at: www.randomhouse.co.uk/offices.htm

THE RANDOM HOUSE GROUP Limited Reg. No. 954009

A CIP catalogue record for this book is available from the British Library.

Printed and bound in Great Britain by Clays Ltd, St Ives plc

To my wife, Joanie:

You're the Ace of my heart's suit of cards.

From the song "The Province of Ledger Domaine," by Charlie Price

Writing this book has been a most collaborative process. My wife has reviewed it countless times. I am grateful for her intelligence, commitment, and stamina! My daughter has been a sharp and humorous resource. The book would never have achieved its current shape without the brilliance and diligence of my editor, Ms. Deborah Brodie. Her fine eye and wit, her deft guidance and encouragement have been invaluable.

Mr. Chris Crutcher provided the heart and motivation for this project, and I am forever in his debt (as he will no doubt remind me). Celeste White, one of my favorite authors, has consistently inspired me with her marvelous craftsmanship and nurturing. Without the perspicacity and support of Melinda Brown, I would not have begun this process in the first place. Serious readers and writers like Kit Anderton and Bill Seimer have contributed regularly. Friends, including Carolyn Warnemuende, Sharon Brisolera, and Kate Anderton, have provided timely suggestions and advocacy.

I have received crucial technical assistance from Ron Parton, clinical division chief, Shasta County Mental Health; Captain Tom Bosenko, Shasta County Sheriff's Office; retired sergeant Dan Kupski, Redding Police Department; Manuel J. Garcia, attorney; Lucy Rogers, RN, BSN; Paul B. Swinderman, MD; and Dr. Steve Hudgens.

Further, I am grateful to my agent, Ms. Tracey Adams, for her professional knowledge and superior negotiation skills.

For your generous help, I thank you, one and all.

—C.P.

The wait of the dead was the loneliest thing Nikki could ever have imagined. Lonelier than thinking her friends were making fun of her. Lonelier than sitting by herself in the gym on a bottom bleacher while others danced.

Maybe she could endure the loneliness if she wasn't so angry—furious really.

He took her and hid her and no one would ever know what had happened. No one would find her. And the years would move away like a train abandoning a station. The tracks becoming covered with weeds, disappearing, with no one to stop there again.

Do the dead cry? Do they ache in sorrow? Do they weep in helpless frustration?

You know they do.

I'll be ready to die right after high school. Join my friends. Edwin, 1953, polio, says he was glad to die. He's a very nice guy and he was super in math. But he hated that iron lung. Get it over with, he says.

That's the way I feel, too. Mom doesn't really need me. I don't have a job. I don't drive.

Kids at school tease me about my name, Murray. Say it's expired, like out of date. And I don't know how they found out about my mom. Maybe some kid's parent saw it in the paper when she was arrested for prostitution. She didn't have to go to jail. And they ride me about my face. I've spent time looking in the mirror. I don't think I'm so ugly. I've had some trouble with my pimples, but I bet everybody has to work on their pimples once in a while.

Blessed Daughter, Born 1966, tells me not to worry. She says I'm cool anyway, but she doesn't realize the way kids in my classes rag on me. She says I'll grow out of it, but she died when she was eleven, brain tumor, so I don't think she's really an expert.

She's smart, though. She tells me what to say to the guys who tease me about my looks or my mother. "Don't get too close, I have AIDS." Cool, huh? They leave me alone now, which is fine with me.

My best friend is probably Dearly.

DEARLY BELOVED.
BORN 1944   DIED 1969
IN BEAUTY REPOSE.

Car wreck, she told me. When she accepted the date, she didn't know he drank so much. She smelled it on his breath the minute she opened her front door. She stayed dry, not sure if she'd have to drive after the party. They didn't get that far. They hit a tree. He broke his neck. She went through the convertible's windshield and bled to death.

Dearly Beloved was perky. She brushed her hair and put on makeup in the filling station where she made him stop before the accident. She even considered taking off her underwear and putting it in her purse, but she was glad she hadn't, after what happened. He was a business manager for a national fraternity. Kappa Chi. He had long fingers.

They are not graveyards. I hate it when people say that. They are cemeteries. The one I know best is Forest Grove. I spend most of my time there. That's where most of my friends are. I don't spend much time with the older people. I figure they deserved it. Not *deserved* it, really, but what could they expect? After forty, you're going to die. The ones my age and the children, they almost all need someone to talk to. I comfort them the best I can. They weren't ready. They'll tell you that. They're not jealous or mean or scary like you might think. Just really lonely. Everybody needs a friend. Even James.

JAMES MCNAUGHTON
TAKEN IN HIS BLOOM
NEVER FORGOTTEN
BORN 1900   DIED 1918

I figure the war got him. He doesn't talk to me yet.

3

I think of myself as The Comforter. That's what I want on my stone.

If I do kick, I'll be the first Kiefer to have graduated from high school in California. That's the promise I made to Mom, my obligation. She won't miss me. I'm more in the way than anything.

Mr. Janochek, the groundskeeper, has been real nice to me, but he still asks me to leave when they lock the front gate at nine at night. I tell him sure, and head out, but he knows I don't leave. I don't have to be home until eleven on weeknights, if then, and I don't have to come home at all Friday and Saturday. Mom thinks I'm out partying because that's what she does.

I don't even need a flashlight anymore. I know where the tree roots are that stick up between the shadier tombstones. Plus, real late at night and early, early morning are the best times to visit. It's super quiet. Easy to hear. Easy to concentrate. Nobody having a funeral or mowing or planting flowers. No cars. They don't even unlock the gate until eight in the morning, and if the weather's bad, sometimes I have the whole place pretty much to myself.

I have kind of a schedule. I start with the youngest because I figure they need the most company. I have about five or ten friends. I don't really count James, yet. And lately I've been hearing a new person, but I can't seem to locate the grave.

Or maybe I could be The Listener. That's better than "The Comforter." Jeez, *comforter* sounds like a bed cover. The Listener. That's mystic.

Two lines. It's all even and everything. I'm pretty sure Dearly will like it.

In about three or four years, you ought to come see me. Ask Mr. Janochek where "The Listener" plot is. He'll know. He keeps all the stuff looking good. He's probably the one who'll find me. He'll understand. I bet you anything.

Deputy Gates was over twenty years with the Sierra County Sheriff's Department out of Riverton, California. He was familiar with sorrow. His wife was long gone, a casualty of his earlier love affair with gambling. His son was dead, two years this coming August, from a speedball overdose the summer before he was going to be the starting middle linebacker on the high school football team. A mistake, Gates hoped . . . an accident, he prayed.

Shortly after his wife left, Gates resigned from the Sheriff's Department and began an even faster slide downhill. Spending nearly every night in casinos, he bet away his house and the rest of his savings. He borrowed until he wiped out his pension, and then was arrested during an altercation with a loan broker. A trip to his own jail embarrassed him enough to start an ongoing recovery process with Twelve-Step meetings.

Now, years later, he sat in his car at Whiskeytown Lake in the foothills west of Riverton, California. The area was at the end of the Central Valley, dry and hot as a griddle through the summers, even though it was surrounded by mountains. Thankfully, it was winter now, and the temperature, fifty-five degrees, made the November day comfortable.

Sitting, quiet, thinking, Gates saw quail families combing through the manzanita. Saw a jack raise its ears as it hesitated to leave its crumple of boulders and chance open ground.

He wondered why he had stayed with investigating. Morbid curiosity? A bitter upbringing that led to foolish notions of power and justice? A uniform that extended playing cowboy into adulthood? He knew he backslid into the job as a sheriff's investigator after his son's death. But not even the domestic violence, the senseless vandalism, the unsolved crimes, and the occasional gore could drive him to civilian work.

He smelled the diesel of a tour bus in the parking lot behind him and heard the faint rumbling as its engine idled. For the hundredth time that week, he thought about the missing Parker girl.

On a rainy evening, October 17, Nikki Parker had left the school gym when cheerleading practice was over, about 6:00. She said good-bye to the woman faculty advisor and to her teammates, who were discussing which four girls made the sturdiest pyramid bottom for a football game stunt. She was always second from the top, so she didn't care what they decided.

Investigators assume that she left the gym and walked downhill toward the parking lot, where she had put her car that morning. The car still sat there the following day, and there was no evidence that she had reached it.

Police surmised that someone she knew had offered her a ride in the evening rain, and she got in with them and disappeared off the face of the earth. The high school grounds were grid-searched by hundreds of law enforcement personnel and volunteers. Not a trace. A list of her closer acquaintances was made, anyone she might have accepted a ride from, and all were interviewed and alibis checked. All school administrative, teaching, maintenance, food service, and transportation employees were interviewed and checked. No one could find an eyewitness to her activity once she left the gym.

The police suspect list was topped by her ex-boyfriend, Rudy, a nineteen-year-old who had dropped out of her high school a year before. He had given up his senior year to travel and work on the cars in his uncle's racing team.

Some said that, after he got back last summer, he ganged up with the town's main conduit for Southern California skag, a small group of bright, disaffected kids from wealthy families who could afford to ride Harleys and have "Dragoons" embroidered on the back of their lambskin jackets. Some said they were his boyhood friends, but that he wasn't really running with them. At any rate, he didn't have an alibi for the 6:00 to 7:00 time slot that day. Nikki's girlfriends thought he was really handsome and sometimes really mean, and that she probably would have gotten into a car with him.

Rudy's statement stank with bravado. "You know what *you* were doing two days ago, 6:00 to 7:00? Somebody says they know that, they probably did whatever you're asking about. I'm busy. I'm doing things all the time. I was with friends doing something. That's all I got. You know what else? I loved that girl. Anybody hurt her, I'd kill them myself, no shit. Give me a few days. I'll figure out what I was doing."

Next on the police favorites list was a young man named John Turner, who was Nikki's private tennis coach and trainer. He was seen as a marginal citizen who made his money by supplying a variety of needs for his all-female clientele. He was tan, facile, and few men who met him trusted him. Many of Nikki's friends, however, thought he was a "hottie."

Nikki's parents paid for the court lessons and the training. They had no idea about the man's character or how much time their daughter actually spent with him. "She has her own car, you know. She's away from home several hours a day and that's the way it is with all the girls now," her mother had told the investigating officer. Everyone thought she would get in a car with him if he invited her.

Turner was glib. "Of course I know Nikki, but I haven't set eyes on her since her lesson last week. She didn't show up for this week's," he told the investigating officer. "I don't have one bit of useful information for you and my next lesson is in fifteen minutes, so if you're through . . . ?"

The third candidate was an overweight school bus driver with a comb-over who should have been right in that area at the same time Nikki exited the front of the gymnasium building. The man, Buell Nostrum, had no criminal record, but word around the school was that he took a strong interest in pretty girls, trying to engage them in conversation, reaching to help them down the bus steps. Administrators were aware of Nostrum's interest but no formal complaint had been filed by either students or parents, and no administrative action had been taken. His supervisor suspected him of fudging time cards and stealing tools occasionally from the vehicle maintenance barn but could never marshal the hard evidence necessary to fire him.

Nostrum's story was that he didn't even know the girl. Possibly true because she never took the bus and he never drove for school sports functions. Police weren't able to confirm whether or not he attended games where he would have seen her cheerlead. He denied it and his wife corroborated. He said he had been doing errands that night and had gone the opposite direction out of the maintenance yard where he routinely parked.

"I didn't go out front at all. I was headed to that big Shopko out on Lake Boulevard. That's why I was late getting home, and you can ask my wife."

Police did. And she confirmed it. A search of the house turned up shopping bags from that market but no recent receipts to confirm dates of purchase.

At the end of October, investigators were left with a missing person, three possible suspects, and not a shred of viable evidence indicating what had actually happened. The parents could afford a $50,000 reward, and the community raised an additional $25,000 to go on top of it. The community organized bloodhound searches of every park and forest area within reason. Ponds and rivers were dragged, and scuba divers went deep into the two local lakes.

Over two thousand man-hours and nobody found a thing.

Pearl didn't think about things. If your Dad worked in a cemetery, would you think about things? Death just around the corner? Nope. She'd save her thinking for homework. She was a private person, and those backbiting queen bees in her classes weren't going to get a shred of personal information to use against her. She had a few friends but none she really trusted. School didn't feel safe in that way.

Today she didn't care about school. She was focused on that dorky kid who talked to graves. She knew he had seen her a couple of times, but he didn't know that she had actually heard him talking to the headstones.

She knew he was spending nearly all his time after school here. She knew that two or three times a week, her dad had to ask him to leave at nine, when he locked the gate. Her dad was the groundskeeper for the Forest Grove Cemetery. He didn't dig graves or anything gross like that, but he managed the landscaping, arranged the burials, and sold new plots to families who needed a pretty place to bury somebody.

Her dad did a nice job with the flowers and even the road. He blew leaves and weeds off the lanes and kept the vines off the big metal gates. Pearl liked the funny stone houses where some families put their relatives, and all the different types of crosses and the statues of angels and saints that watched over everybody. When she died, she wouldn't mind being put here. But she wouldn't want that kid sitting over her and talking. She was certain about that.

Pearl decided to bust him while he was doing his thing

with the graves. She would let him know he wasn't fooling anybody, let him know she was the boss in this cemetery. She knew he was usually just down the hill in the late afternoon. Since her dad was still working, this was the perfect time.

She left the cottage, being careful the screen door didn't slam, walked quietly down the road and right up behind where he sat in front of a tombstone, and said, "They're dead, you know!" He jumped about a foot, which wasn't easy from a sitting position.

He started stammering at her. Totally irritating. She told him to calm down or she'd make her dad tell him to leave. Then she got mad at herself. *Here's a ninth grader going to get her dad to come help her!*

"What are you doing talking to a headstone?"

"I'm not talking to a headstone." He was looking at her like *she* was the idiot.

"You're talking to yourself?" she asked.

"No."

"Well?" she said. She had her hands on her hips like a traffic cop.

"It's really none of your business," he said, turning his back to her.

"Everything that happens here is my business," she told him. "My dad runs this place."

"You're Janochek's kid?" he blurted, surprising the heck out of her.

"How do you know his name?"

"What's your name?" he asked, before she could get back on top of things.

"Pearl." *Shoot!* She wanted to go on the offensive. "I've seen you slinking around here, day after day"—shaking her head like he was beyond help—"You're just a goofy grave sniffer!" *There. That's more like it.*

Murray gave up hoping she would just leave. He turned to face her. Pearl was standing right up close to him, looking belligerent.

"Damn it! Don't you have any manners?" He was losing patience.

"Me? I'm not the one creeping around a cemetery like a body snatcher. It's supposed to be quiet and dignified here."

Murray skidded back and forth between anger and amusement. He hated being talked to in that tone of voice, but on the other hand, she was kind of cute, trying to be so tough with her bad-guy pose, and at the same time leaking a smile at the corners of her mouth.

"I am not bothering you. Go do whatever it is you do and leave me alone!"

"No."

"No . . . ?" He was getting tired of this game.

"Tell me what you're doing."

"You'll just keep hassling me."

"No, I won't," Pearl said, taking her hands off her hips and softening her expression. "I'm not really trying to hurt your feelings. I just kind of like messing with you."

"Can you see that I don't like it?"

"Yeah, but you'll get used to it. I'm a lot of fun to be around."

Murray barked a laugh in spite of himself. "Who told you that?"

"My dad."

"Jeez, he *has* to say stuff like that. You're his kid."

"No, he means it."

Murray massaged his forehead. "You'll just tell and I'll get in trouble and everything will get screwed up."

Pearl looked him right in the eye. "Are you doing something bad?"

"No. No! It's nothing like that. You'd never understand in a million years."

Pearl took a half step toward him. "Hey. I'm sorry I scared you and acted, like, so tough. Tell me what you're doing. Please."

Murray looked at her. She was probably thirteen or fourteen. She had a curly blond tangle of hair and she wore overalls with a colored T-shirt underneath a faded jean jacket. She wasn't wearing makeup. Her brown walking shoes were scuffed. She had a decent face with straight teeth and a smudge of dirt near her chin. She smelled like woodsmoke from her dad's workshop stove. Her face now held a sincere pleading look that begged to be trusted.

"No," he said. He saw the way her face fell and felt a quick pang. "No," he repeated, more softly.

Pearl turned and stomped away before he could say more.

Back up the hill, she stormed into the workshop and slammed the door. She didn't respond to her father's offer of ham sandwiches and coleslaw, didn't say a word as she passed through the back door and walked into the small two-bedroom cottage the cemetery provided as housing. She went to her room and closed the door. She tore her jean jacket off and threw it at the wall by her bed, hitting the poster of Cheryl Miller coaching during a timeout in a WNBA game and the one beside it of Haley Joel Osment in *The Sixth Sense*. She loved his movie with Robert Duvall. The posters rattled with the jacket's impact but neither fell.

That wack . . . that stupid dick! She was too mad to sit. She'd fix that kid. Count on it!

He had been watching those kids, Pearl and the Kiefer boy, and thought, *God, how did any of us ever make it to adults?* Pearl was acting tough, like a bouncer, and Kiefer looked like he just wanted to be left in peace. Fat chance, now that he was on her radar. Pearl made Canyon's freshman girls' basketball team because she was what the coach called aggressive, tenacious on defense. Once she started something, she didn't let go easily. He loved to watch her fight the taller girls for rebounds.

He thought Pearl had reason to be angry; mad that he had married her mom instead of someone stable, mad that her mom ignored her, mad that she was an only child living in a cemetery instead of a neighborhood with other kids.

Janochek had tried to talk with her about some of these things, but since she'd been eleven, talking hadn't gone so well. So he just tried to be polite and put food on the table. She didn't want to ride bikes or go to movies with him on the weekends anymore. He wished that she got invited to sleepovers or had a group of girlfriends who called her.

He knew she was embarrassed by his work. And he wondered if kids teased her about being a ghoul. He told her if anyone made fun of her or gave her trouble, he would come to school and bite them on the neck.

He knew that the Kiefer kid hung around the cemetery nearly every night. Murray Kiefer. What a name to be saddled with. Kiefer's mom reminded Janochek a little of Pearl's mom. Vera Kiefer was a party girl, and she hooked up with different men who would keep her in food, liquor, and rent for a couple of weeks at a time. He could make a pretty cold comparison with his dead wife, Doreen. He thought he probably should have divorced her when Pearl was a toddler so she wouldn't have had to watch her mom self-destruct, running off with other men for days at a time, until leukemia ended her life. Before it was over, Pearl wound up mothering *her*.

Odd to think how maybe one of the safest places to be anymore was a cemetery. Murray was thin and gawky; hell, even his hair was thin and gawky. At first, Janochek thought the boy was smoking dope and tripping when he stuck around the cemetery, but by now, he knew Kiefer was just hanging out and talking to himself. And, really, what was the matter with that? Janochek did that some when he was a kid. Made up all kinds of fantasy games. He felt sorry for the kid. Thought him harmless.

Janochek was curious what was going to happen if Pearl started pestering the boy. He didn't want his daughter to run the boy out just for target practice. Pearl reminded him of a cat he had once who was really sleek and lovely, very clever, cuddly most of the time, but had a mean streak that was unpredictable, and every so often, Janochek would get mauled when he wasn't paying attention.

Murray better watch out. Janochek knew Pearl was steaming. Usually, it was just sports, homework, solitary games, and fiction books for her. No major moody drama unless he asked her to clean her room. But tonight she was seething and wouldn't talk about it. During dinner, when he brought it up, she changed the subject rather cleverly, asking

17

him a question about the history of cemeteries, which she knew from past experience was one of his favorite topics, one he could talk on and on about.

"Tell me again, Dad, who invented cemeteries? I'm probably going to write a paper on it at school." She was so transparent. But it worked. Or, he gave up and let it work.

"Well, you know, honey, that when human beings started burying their dead, they usually marked the graves with a heavy stone or a stack of rocks, apparently believing the weight would keep the dead from rising."

He warmed to the topic. "Later on, words or pictures were added to the rocks or pieces of wood to commemorate the person's life or to serve as a locator like today's tombstones. As people became less nomadic, or maybe wealthier, the graves got fancier."

He reminded her of the pictures she had seen, big tombs like the Taj Mahal and the pyramids. He told her that the so-called modern cemeteries didn't get started until after holy people's bones and relics began to be kept in temples or churches, and that practice probably led to wealthy people paying to get buried in those places so they would be close at hand when the call to heaven came.

She was keeping eye contact and he was encouraged by her attention. "The less wealthy religious people wanted to get buried as close to church as possible for the same reason and so they were put in the churchyards." He emphasized that, as time passed, they had to be stacked pretty much on top of each other when space became scarce.

"Remember," he said, "the east side of the church was preferred, as close to the building as possible, so those folks would be the first to see the sunrise on Judgment Day. The north corner border was the least favored."

He shook his head. "Some even thought the Devil lurked there, and that's where they usually put the strangers to the community, the stillborn, the suicides, if they let them in at all, and the illegitimate children—"

"I'm not one of those, am I, Dad?" Pearl broke in.

"No, honey," he said, "not yet," and they both smiled at his silliness.

He plowed on. "Anyway, it wasn't until the 1700s that churches in some European countries just plain and simple ran out of room."

He could see that her eyes were beginning to glaze over, but he couldn't stop himself.

"In eighteenth-century Paris—"

Pearl interrupted, "Thanks a lot, Dad. I'm finished eating and I've got to go write this stuff down before I forget it." She whisked her glass and dish to the sink and was off to her room before he got his mouth closed.

Billup didn't like the kid lurking around the graveyard. He had wanted to get even with the little freak since that day he had interfered with Billup's interrogation of his mother, Vera. He hadn't known the kid was home. He was in the slut's living room, slapping her around to get the name of her pimp or escort service. And then he figured she could buy her way out of the bust by giving him some satisfaction. He was just getting on her when the kid came out of the bedroom with a goddamn phone and threatened to call 911 unless Billup left. Standoff. So Billup split, but he knew that sooner or later, he'd get even. In spades. Billup hated to be embarrassed.

As Public Affairs Officer, it was his business to protect the town's moral fiber, to prevent trouble. He'd been keeping tabs on Kiefer for a month. He thought the kid looked like a pervert, but he couldn't prove it. The geek didn't have a juvie sheet. Billup had checked at the school: C grades, no suspensions. Still, Billup believed Kiefer was a sleaze, just like his mama. Acorns and oaks. He would make the little creep pay for obstructing justice. It might take a while, but he would pay. Billup would see to it.

Graveyards. *Give me a break.* The kid was either pulling something or planning something, probably robbing crypts. When Billup talked to the caretaker, Janochek said the kid wasn't digging anything up, wasn't bothering anyone. When Billup rousted the kid on the street outside the cemetery a couple of weeks ago, the boy was clean—no pot odor on his clothes, no pipe or papers. Billup had expected the kid would smell like corpses or sinsemilla.

He saw the boy with Janochek's girl tonight. Nothing but trouble there. Billup remained surprised that Janochek didn't eighty-six that kid and file a report. The man could probably get a restraining order to bar the kid just on weird-ness alone. Made Billup glad he'd never had a child. His boy turned out like that, he'd put him in a sack and throw him in the river.

Billup figured he ought to toss the kid's mama again. Every job deserved a few perks.

He brought another beer out of his cooler and listened to the Kings game out of Sacramento while he waited for Kiefer to double back and climb over the near cemetery wall. He would bust him for trespassing. Nip this little creep in the bud.

Robert Barry Compton had routines. Days he didn't work, he walked his circuit, about five miles round-trip from his residence hotel. Same time every evening, 5:00 to 7:00. It allowed him to feel okay, to hush the voices that had started a few years ago with crank and never quite stopped. He slept through the day, got up and smoked three (always three) cigarettes, ate a couple of Milky Ways for dinner, and then he'd head out. The same path every time. It was like his medicine. On non-workdays, if he didn't walk, he couldn't sleep.

Once he got a good route, he stuck to it. Down Court to Eureka Way, west on Eureka to the high school, through the campus and over to the park, up to Market, a few more blocks and he was home.

Three days a week, he worked fast food. On those days, he felt useful. Often, when he got off work at the new TacoBurger downtown, he would walk over to the Arcade Newsstand, look at some magazines, and then walk two blocks to Morgan's Bargain Emporium, where he'd spend an hour and sometimes a dollar or two browsing through the bins. Or he would walk over to the Rite Aid by his residence hotel. Usually he didn't see anyone he knew by name, and no one said anything to him.

He hated his name. Too boring. He wanted people to call him "Bear" like a nickname for Barry, but they never did. Since they wouldn't, he tried to make everyone call him by his whole name, Robert Barry Compton. *Mister*. Mister Robert Barry Compton.

He was twenty-two years old and skinny, with lank blond hair that he kept chopped off at ear level. He dressed in a faded black ski jacket, a grayish white T-shirt, no-brand jeans, and heavy black stomper boots.

His ears were red and pockmarked from several piercings, but he had lost his studs when he was picked up for disturbing the peace in Chico. The police took them before they put him in the holding tank. By the time they took him to the hospital, he'd forgotten all about them. He meant to get more. He just forgot.

In Rite Aid, he would look at the candy aisle first and then check out the magazines. Just killing time. He would walk around, waiting for something to catch his eye.

That day, he found himself in front of a stationery table looking at Christmas cards: Nativity scenes, snowmen with red wool scarves and top hats, dark blue skies illuminated by huge silver-white stars. Wasn't it too early for Christmas cards? Had there even been Thanksgiving yet? He wasn't sure.

He thought about writing a Christmas card. He was stumped. He couldn't think of a single person to write to. He could probably send one to the hospital back in Chico, but he hated most of the staff and their monotonous speeches about taking medication. Besides, all his friends would be discharged by now. He realized that he didn't know anybody's address, except his mother's, and he was probably going to see her on Christmas Day anyway.

He wouldn't give a card to anybody in his hotel, that's for sure. A bunch of 'tards and mummies. He didn't even talk to them. There was nobody near his age.

And he didn't really need to get his mom anything. He had already gotten her something. For her birthday. But her birthday had slipped past a while ago and he had missed it. Okay, so she'd get it for Christmas. He couldn't remember what he'd bought her, now that he thought about it. Scarf . . . perfume . . . . Nope, it wouldn't come to him. And Mr. Robert Barry Compton began to feel just a little bit mad. Forgetting things made him feel stupid, and he just couldn't stand that.

There was something else Robert really needed to remember. It happened a while ago and it was just on the edge of his mind, but he couldn't call it up. It was important. He remembered that much. He had made a vow to do something. What? Damn it! He could feel his face getting warmer. *Weirdo! Crazy bastard! Good-for-nothing!* Some guys had called him that in high school and he could still hear them saying it.

He noticed he was stuffing a Christmas card down the front of his pants. He was going to steal it, just like he had taken those sex magazines yesterday at the newsstand. He slowly glanced from side to side to see if he was being observed. Nobody was paying him any attention. He pushed the card down below his belt line and felt himself stiffen a little down there. It always felt really good to steal. Maybe he'd go down to the newsstand after he left this store.

He wondered which card he had chosen. He told himself to go to a couple of other counters to throw off suspicion before leaving. He browsed some paperbacks and some teen magazines before walking out. No buzzers went off.

Outside, the air was chilled, and he felt his muscles tighten with the cold. He felt strong, even a little tough. He

24

decided to go out back behind the stores in the mall and look through the boxes and Dumpsters. Like a street warrior. Like somebody who lived on his own because he chose to. Took what he wanted. Lived off stupid rich people's discards.

He was opening a Dumpster lid when a stock clerk came out of a back door to toss some cardboard boxes. The clerk hesitated when he saw Robert holding the lid and gave him the eye. Robert pulled a board from a broken packing crate. The clerk went back inside, closed the door, and locked it. Robert threw his board at the door. Jeez, he'd never done that before. It felt great. That must be why kids shoot people at schools, he thought. Because it feels so good.

He dropped the lid and walked quickly out the back lot, heading toward a gas station. I should steal a car, he thought. But he went into the bathroom on the side of the building instead, opened the stall door and sat on the toilet. The crunch the Christmas card made inside his pants surprised him. Just as well, he thought, tearing it into strips and dropping it in the bowl. For the second time that day, he wondered if he should shave his head.

Murray again heard a voice that was different from the others. After his confrontation with the girl, he had been meandering along the side lanes, trying to get rid of his irritation. He went as far as the cemetery boundary and was returning on the next lane when he noticed the sound. He began placing his feet carefully, his sneakers cushioning each step, so that no noise would interfere with his listening.

He couldn't tell much. The voice was really faint and muddled with groans or wind or something. He thought he heard ". . . him me . . . fine me . . . plea . . ." A soft wail, like a pet whimpering alone in a car. He wondered if maybe it was from that girl who lived with Mr. Janochek, playing a trick on him. Could she have screwed his mind up, fouled up his receiving? He looked around but saw no sign of her.

Murray gave up listening and went directly to the Chandler plot to get in contact with Dearly. She started.

"So, now maybe you have girl trouble, Sugar?"

"No. It's nothing like that. She's the caretaker's kid and she's rude and really nosey. I was just wondering if she got in my mind somehow and messed up my connections."

"Well, I'm reading you loud and clear."

Murray could see Dearly just like she was right before the crash. She wore this tight purple woolly skirt and sweater and had a pretty linen handkerchief she fiddled with, pulled and twisted in her hands like worry beads. And she was so beautiful with her permed brown hair and red lipstick.

"How are you going to deal with the holiday vacation?" she asked.

"I already figured I'd tell Mom I was going to spend a lot of time over at a friend's house. I don't think she'll care. Have you noticed anything strange around here lately?"

"Like what?"

"I don't know. Like a person who isn't even dead. Or somebody new. Or somebody who's lost?"

"I'm pretty sure there's a lot of lost souls in this place. Your guy James, for example, what's with him?"

"No, I mean something really different."

"No, honey, can't say as I have, but I'll keep an ear open. Don't worry. Me and Blessed have got this place covered."

He always asked Dearly if there was anything he could do for her, and she always said, "Just wildflowers. Every spring, just some wildflowers. Lupine or ceanothus to go with my outfit."

Blessed was his next stop. Murray sat down at the side of Blessed's stone and took a deep breath to help him listen better. She was such a cool girl. He bet if she had lived, she would be a doctor or a college professor by now. He was having a little trouble hearing, so he moved right in front of her headstone and sat down close enough to touch the carved dates.

"Tell me again. I missed it," he said, leaning forward a little.

"I said, I think you should give that girl a chance. She came to see you, you know. How many girls have done that lately?"

"She's rude, Blessed. She's a brat . . . and bossy and looking for a fight."

"She seems pretty bright to me. And you know what? I think underneath that attitude, she might be a little lonely and looking for a friend. How many other people spend most of their afternoons in a cemetery?"

"I don't need any more friends. I've got all of you."

"Think it over. You know I'm right."

Blessed was always sure of herself. Murray kept seeing her in her hospital gown. He wanted to picture what she wore, like when she went to school, but all he could get were awful loud colors, oranges and lime greens, and blouses covered with tiny amoeba shapes. She liked to chew that sugarless gum. He knew that, and he knew she stuck it under her dining room table at home while her dad was saying the blessing before dinner.

It was time to ask her.

"Have you heard anything new around here lately?"

"You mean a joke or something?"

"No. I . . . I thought I heard a new person, or a lost person yesterday . . . but it might just have been Janochek's kid messing with me. I thought I heard someone say 'him me.' And then 'fine me.' It was pretty faint and kind of garbled. I couldn't tell if it was an adult or a kid, or even if they were from here."

"Huh. Where were you when you heard it?"

"I don't know. I mean I was here . . . in the cemetery. I was walking around near the road from the main gate through the front part, kind of on my way to Dearly's place."

"The new part of the cemetery they opened a couple of years ago?"

"I don't know when they opened it. It's the place where

they're putting the people that didn't have older family plots, I guess."

"You think it comes from there?"

"I don't know. Maybe."

"You should check it out."

"You think I should walk by every stone around there and see if I pick anything up?"

"Up to you, Grunge Puppy!" That got them started, and while they were teasing each other, he decided that tomorrow he would walk very carefully all around that newer section. Get to the bottom of this. Maybe make a new friend.

Mr. Robert Barry Compton was standing beside the deep fryer, waiting for the next batch of fries to get done. He had on the paper hat that he hated wearing and he was scowling. The manager had already talked to him twice about his "negative facial expressions." What a do-right! Robert felt like it was his *own* damn face. He ought to be able to do what he wanted with it. Actually, though, the manager's comment surprised him. He wasn't aware he was scowling.

Like today. He was just standing there, trying to remember. That's one of the things the meds or the crank really screwed up, his memory. Anyway, he was trying to remember two things. One, did he take his Risperdal this morning? And two, what was it that he was going to tell somebody? He had some information about something. He remembered again yesterday on his walk. He was going to tell somebody something that might be important, but he couldn't quite dredge it up.

"Compton! Fries are smokin'!"

"Okay, okay, I got it."

Crap. Maybe it would come to him later.

It did.

Robert Barry was absentmindedly putting cheese, onions, and hot sauce on four chalupas in a rack, looking out the drive-through window at the lunch line. Cars. Cars! What he had been trying to remember had something to do with cars. A car. He was sure of it. What kind of car? What color? Why did he make some vow about it? Those things he couldn't recall just yet, but it was a start! But right away, he was feeling sad again. He would forget it. He knew he would, and then he would be back where he started.

He did his personal test. He pictured his weekly pill organizer, clear plastic with blue letters for each day of the week over each compartment. After he woke up, did he go to the box that he kept on his dresser and take today's dose? *Shit!* He did. He knew it, but was it today or yesterday?

Bang! He had a flash! God, he loved it when he had a new idea, clear and strong and important. He took out his wallet and withdrew his Social Security card.

"Chalupas up! Hey, Compton! Chalupas up!" The window guy with the headphones was yelling at him.

Robert Barry stifled his reflex to yell, *Screw you, do-right!* That would probably cost him this job, and his rent was coming up.

"Yeah, okay." He figured that bought him at least thirty seconds while he took out his ballpoint and scribbled "car" on the back of his Social Security card. There, he thought with satisfaction, now I got something going! And then he finished the damn chalupas and walked them over to the creep at the window.

When Billup represented the department at public functions, he was supposed to look his best. He always folded his suit jacket lining to the outside before laying it over the seat of his motor-pool Ford. He put on a clean white shirt every work morning, freshly pressed with just a touch of starch. Sometimes he shaved against the grain so close his face chapped. He used hair oil that showed his comb marks all day long and he used an expensive deodorant from Macy's that doubled as cologne. He was always prepared for someone to notice him. *People take one look at me, they know I take care of business.* But most people didn't seem to look at him at all.

He never got the recognition he deserved. He never got the breaks. His high school football coach had told him right to his face that Billup was good, but he wasn't big enough. "I never start short players," the coach told him on the sidelines of the practice field after Billup had asked for more playing time. "They don't intimidate." Billup stuck it out anyway, but he rarely got in the games.

He didn't get asked to dances, didn't make friends with other guys. The girls he asked out usually seemed to have prior commitments. He figured maybe it was his breath, but his mother had reassured him. Secretly, he thought other people were just jealous of him. He was smart, savvy, and hardworking, and they just used their phony charm to get by.

His frustration already had his stomach growling. No sense fueling that fire. Getting pissed off always made him start drinking, and it was still three hours till the end of his shift. He knew he had been drinking a lot lately, and he knew that when he got loaded, he was more likely to hassle a prostitute or some parked teenagers, and he knew that was risky. The hooker might be connected or the kids might have a political parent. Plus, lately he had been blacking out more, losing nights, sometimes a whole weekend. *Got to be careful!*

He started his car and made a U-turn, heading for the south end of town. He would do some service work instead. Show up at the mission. Ask what the police department could do to help the staff with the homeless.

He wouldn't bust the kid for cruising the graveyard, at least not today. Leave him alone for now. Besides, he didn't want a city beat patrol logging that he seemed to be staking out the graveyard on a regular basis. Might bring unnecessary questions.

Murray left the cemetery that night without searching any farther and arrived home just after dark. His mother was sitting on the couch with a man Murray did not recognize, rubbing the man's neck and shoulders.

"Oh, hi, honey," she greeted him. "You know Eric, here, don't you? Say hello to Eric."

Murray looked at both of them. His mom was wearing some kind of drapey thin robe, and Eric looked like he had just come off a shift at the paper mill: brown jeans, tan crepe-soled work boots, plaid shirt with a gray T-shirt underneath. Eric was staring at the TV. Didn't bother to look up. Murray continued to his room without speaking.

His mother added, "There's half a cheeseburger and some fries on the counter and you can put 'em in the oven if you're hungry." But by the time she had finished the sentence, he had already closed his door and could no longer hear her.

Murray woke up the next morning, still dressed, lying on his bed on top of the covers. He thought immediately about the Janochek girl. *Why is this so upsetting?* He stood up and listened for his mom and Eric. Nothing. It was after eight. If Eric had spent the night, he would probably already have gone to work. *Blood is thicker than water.* His mom had drummed that into his head, attempting to reassure him that, in the end, he was more important to her than the different men she saw.

Murray put himself on autopilot, took a shower, and got ready for school. He couldn't recall if he was supposed to have done any homework. He grabbed his backpack and went to the kitchenette. He ate a banana and made a sack lunch of potato chips and raisins. He looked for a small can of juice, any kind, but the ones in the fridge had already been opened. He looked in the cupboard: some cans of chicken noodle soup and chili. A jar of unopened dill pickles. He gave up and looked for some loose change. When he had gathered seventy-five cents, he pocketed it to buy a drink later, and left the house, making sure he locked the door. He was real mad at his mom, but still, he didn't want anything to happen to her.

As he walked toward school, he was afraid that this mess with the girl was going to wreck his haven at the cemetery. He knew he couldn't stand to be cut off from Dearly and Blessed. They had become like family. And who would comfort the others? He knew he had made a mistake yesterday. He had to make friends with the girl to ensure his place in the cemetery. He decided to appear harmless and boring, and then maybe she'd feel a little sorry for him, lose interest, and leave him alone. When she got back from school today, he'd find her and apologize.

Around noon, Gates finished taking statements regarding a theft of chemistry equipment at a private school outside the city limits. He had spoken to school officials and then to three classes of students, but he had his own idea about the robbery. The county roads within a five-mile radius of the school had hundreds of rundown shacks hidden in thickets of manzanita. Recent brush fires in the area suggested some folks might be doing some outdoor cooking . . . of ephedrine. Notoriously easy to make small batches of meth. He was willing to bet somebody had just replenished their manufacturing equipment at the school's expense. He would be surprised later in the week to find that it was the teacher herself and her new boyfriend doing the cooking.

He got in his car, ready for a break, and drove to a small nearby reservoir high enough to have a view of the Riverton area. The older he got, the more he noticed how beautiful scenery soothed him. Now the snow atop Mount Shasta flashed like a mirror in the winter sun and the impoundment's ripples shuffled against reedy banks where blackbirds rested. A solitary osprey scanned the water's surface for a midday meal.

Gates believed that if he could put enough wit and determination into investigating the Parker girl's disappearance, what happened would make sense.

The girl had no reason to run away, and no one who knew her thought she had. Barring a witness who came forward or a surprise confession, he was going to cast a wider net. He wasn't going to let this drop.

He was surprised by his next thought. *When we figure this one out, I'm going to go after what happened to my son. I'm going to learn whether it was an accident or a suicide, and I'm going to live with that information and get on with the rest of my life . . . maybe even start dating again.*

Those unbidden thoughts released strong feelings. He slowed his breathing, put his attention back on the water. He looked at the rills and scallops the breeze made on the surface. Shortly, he got a sense of what was troubling him in the case file.

The Riverton police had asked the boyfriend, the tennis coach, and the bus driver to voluntarily surrender their cars for inspection. They were told it would enable the police to eliminate them as suspects. All three agreed. Nothing turned up. Gates felt certain Nikki must have gotten into somebody's car. Could one of them have borrowed a car? Did this situation really indicate that degree of planning? There was no evidence, no report of anyone loitering near the gym in the days prior. The perpetrator would have had to have been incredibly lucky to pick her up at an exact moment when there were no witnesses.

He made a decision to explore whether any of the three suspects was in the habit of borrowing or driving different vehicles. Gates would check it out, but he didn't believe it. He was troubled by what he did believe, by what he was aware of more strongly than ever. *This crime was chance. It wasn't planned. It was opportunity. And we might never have a clue to the identity of the real perpetrator.*

As she waited for the school bus, Pearl went over her idea for getting even with the Kiefer kid. This morning at breakfast, she had asked her dad again what the guy's name was, and he had told her. Murray Kiefer. He also told her to leave him alone. Said the boy was harmless and not to bug him.

Pearl knew that her dad often didn't know what was good for him—case in point, marrying her mom. She knew her dad just had some misplaced sympathy for this creep and that he wouldn't let himself realize that Kiefer's messing around was probably driving decent family members and mourners away from the cemetery. Sooner or later, they would probably complain about the job her dad was doing. She was going to save him from himself. And the Kiefer kid? She was going to fry him for the way he treated her when she was just trying to be nice.

She knew that a city cop sometimes parked outside the cemetery in the afternoon near the gate, and she had seen him talking with Kiefer before. What if she told the cop that Kiefer had tried to touch her butt yesterday when they were talking? That would get him in trouble and out of there quick, even if he denied it.

She boarded the yellow bus when it pulled up and chose a seat by herself near the front. If she played the butt card and her dad found out, he'd be real mad, especially after his warning, so she'd have to tell the cop not to involve her dad. Would he anyway? Yeah, probably.

She considered pushing some of the tombstones over and blaming it on Kiefer, but she wasn't sure she was strong enough to do that. She thought of defacing some of the stones with a marking pen or spray paint and blaming it on Kiefer, but that could possibly backfire and get her dad in trouble. She thought of stealing some tools from her dad's workshop and planting them in Kiefer's backpack. That would make her dad feel betrayed by the kid and angry enough to give him the boot. Maybe even report him to the police.

That's what she would do. Take her dad's favorite pen, his multiple screwdriver thing, his special pliers with the red grips that his friend had given him for his birthday, and the paper money from the petty cash box her dad kept on his desk. She would fold them up in a sack and slip it in the guy's pack when he was busy talking to himself.

She could pull it off. She had snuck up on him before. Get him now and get him good!

Robert had awakened late in the afternoon and wondered whether he had taken his pills yet. He walked to his dresser and saw that he had already started his new system. He was keeping a notepad by his medication organizer, and every time he took meds, he was going to write the date and time on the pad, and by God, he would know for sure and certain if he had taken the damn stuff right. His social worker at County had suggested that several times, but now he was finally ready to try it. Sure, he hated the meds, but at least they helped muffle the voices a little bit. *You're a dipshit! Wise up! Fool! You're crazy! Good-for-nothing, good-for-nothing, good-for-nothing!*

The major thing about the meds was that they kept him from having to go back to the hospital. He hated the hospital. Once, when he had been on a three-day crank run, the police had picked him up for running down the middle of the Esplanade screaming. They didn't understand that people were trying to kill him and he was just trying to get away. They put him in the psych ward and strapped him down to a bed so he couldn't get up, and he had never been so scared in his life. He peed himself. He'd almost rather die than go back there.

The meds made him think slower, and he was pretty sure they messed up his memory, but his friends on the unit had convinced him that, if he took them regularly, he wouldn't have to come back to a place like that. If that's what it took, he was willing. Besides, he worked. He had his own money. And one of these days, he'd probably get a girlfriend and a house when he was ready. Much, much better than being locked up.

The notepad said, "11/30, 9:00 a.m." *Alright!* He took his next dose and wrote down, "Ditto, 5:00 p.m." He felt good about himself. *This is working.* He stood still for a moment and listened for voices. Nope. *This is working!*

Pearl could see that Kiefer was waiting for her as she walked through the gate, done with practice for the day. *Shoot!* She hadn't expected that. He was standing between her and the workshop, hands folded in front of him like a sissy. She decided to play it cool for now and spring her plan later in the afternoon.

"Hi," he said when she was about ten feet away.

She didn't say anything.

"Look, I'm sorry about yesterday," he said, keeping eye contact. "I was embarrassed."

She looked like she wanted to say "You didn't seem embarrassed; you seemed more like an asshole," but she held her silence.

"I pray," he said. "I pray for all the dead people, and I thought you'd make fun of me. I'm very religious, and I . . . I want all the dead people to go to heaven, so I come out every day and pray for them. Especially the young—" He bit that off. He didn't want to give her anything she could use against him somehow. She still didn't say anything, didn't seem to believe him.

Finally her expression changed. She fumbled for words.

"Uh, yeah, okay, I see what you mean. Well, you go ahead. I'm sorry if I bothered you." She walked past him and entered the workshop.

He was left standing with his hands still clasped in front. That was a quick turnaround, he thought. She just wants to get rid of me. *Crap!* He turned and went down toward Blessed's grave for solace. He didn't hear or see Pearl two minutes later when she guided the screen door closed so it wouldn't make any noise and followed him with a sack under her arm.

Murray started talking to Blessed before he even sat down.

"I think I really blew it, big time. That little brat is going to mess me up. I can feel it." He knelt right in front of the stone and leaned his head over so he could rest his forehead against it.

"Bet you wished you'd followed my advice, huh? I told you she was just lonely and wanted a friend, but oh no. Now you've hurt her feelings and she's mad and she's gonna get back at you."

"What do you think she's going to do?"

"Something you won't like, I'll bet. She seems like a sharp cookie. She'll come up with something."

"I tried to apologize."

"You fed her a line of bull. I don't think she believed you."

"What should I do now?"

Blessed laughed. "I think you better do what you said. I think you better pray!"

Looking back, he guessed that was when the girl did it. When he was leaning over talking to Blessed. He didn't hear a thing. But then he wasn't listening to that world.

Pearl was sitting in the big green overstuffed chair near the woodstove in the workshop when her dad came in from his afternoon rounds. They said hi to each other and then her dad sat at his desk to check e-mail and respond to the day's invoices. Pearl waited quietly, unable to concentrate on her geography text. After a wait that was long enough to have her doubting her plan, her dad turned toward her.

"Honey, did you borrow my pen for your homework?"

Bingo! "I don't think so. Which one?"

"The black one with the white star on the cap. The one my dad gave me."

"No. I haven't seen it. I wonder, though . . . I'll tell you what I did see."

"What?"

"When I got back from practice, that strange kid was standing up here by the workshop door, looking twitchy. He hardly said anything to me when I said hello, and he hustled off like he was in a hurry to get someplace."

Janochek took off his reading glasses and swiveled in his chair to face his daughter.

"Are you saying that you think the Kiefer boy was in here and took my pen?"

"I don't know. Was the door locked?"

"You tell me. I just got here a few minutes ago."

"I don't know. I didn't really pay any attention."

Pearl was still while Janochek slowly surveyed the room.

"Is there anything else missing?" she asked, more polite than curious.

Janochek looked at her very closely now. All this time, the Kiefer kid had been coming around and nothing had ever been missing. Nothing disturbed in any way.

"Why do you ask?"

"I don't know. Just wondering, I guess."

Janochek swiveled back to his desk. He made a visual inspection, then stood and went over to his workbench and did the same. Right away, he could see the red-handled pliers were missing, and he knew he hadn't taken them anywhere else. His thoughts were divided. One part of him making an inventory of tools; another part thinking about his daughter. The fancy pen, the red-handled pliers. They might have attracted Kiefer's attention. But why? That was the part that didn't compute. Kiefer would know he'd be the first suspect and that he would possibly be evicted from the cemetery, even if he wasn't caught red-handed. He turned again to look at his daughter.

"The red pliers," he said.

"Huh," she said, seeming barely interested. "When I saw him, he looked like he was maybe stuffing some money in his pocket," she added, her face expressionless.

Janochek turned back to the desk and reached for the gray metal petty-cash box he kept on the back left corner. He opened it. Loose change all over the bottom and two or three receipts, but otherwise empty. The forty or fifty dollars it usually held was gone. He set it back on the desk without comment.

"Let's go talk to Kiefer," he said.

Murray was sitting with Edwin. He had asked him the "heard anyone new?" question, and Edwin had said no and then was saying how, when he got polio, the kids he thought were his friends gradually stopped visiting him in the hospital. Though his friends really tried hard to disguise it, he could see their pity, and that hurt. That hurt more than anything. More than his parents' heavy sorrow. Even more than not being able to move his arms and legs. He'd gone from being a friend, an equal, to being a chore people did because they felt sorry for him. The boy he was had disappeared, and there was this tragic dummy in his place.

"Better to die," he was saying.

Murray was thinking that's how he felt sometimes. He had gone as far as he could go. He couldn't even imagine being an adult.

Murray heard them come up behind him. Janochek spoke as soon as he stopped walking, at the foot of Edwin's grave.

"Murray, I need to talk to you for a minute."

Something was wrong. Murray could see it in his face. *She got me!*

"Yes, sir," he said.

"My daughter said she ran into you up by the workshop today. Is that true?"

"Yes, sir."

"I need to ask what you were doing."

Murray's mind was racing. What could she have said?

"Uh, I was waiting for her, your daughter, uh, Pearl . . . I wanted to apologize . . . for yesterday." He could feel himself sweating.

"Apologize?" Janochek said. "For yesterday?" He was clearly puzzled.

"Uh, yeah. She may have told you . . . ." Murray could see she hadn't. He looked over to her. She was just standing there looking back at him. Quiet. Nothing on her face.

"I was maybe a little mean to her." *Be careful!* "She

wanted to know what I was doing at the graves and I didn't want to tell her I was praying. I was embarrassed. I . . . I just brushed her off and I think I hurt . . . I mean I *know* I hurt her feelings." Both the girl and her father were as still as the stone angels on the crypt behind them. *Say more!* "I came up to the workshop today to apologize to her and to tell her I was just praying."

"He's not just praying!" Pearl startled them both.

Murray had an impulse to argue, but he stayed quiet.

Janochek was looking at Pearl but speaking to Murray.

"We've, uh, misplaced some things up in the workshop, and we came down here to ask you if you had seen them anywhere."

He continued to look at Pearl. Murray was stumped. Lost some graves? Misplaced what? Markers? Signs? He couldn't get ahold of what Janochek was asking about. Murray looked at Pearl and saw she was now looking at his backpack. Janochek's gaze followed hers. Murray began to get it.

"You think I took something! You think I took something of yours?" Murray could feel his eyes brim. "Oh, God, I would never do that. I would never do that!"

Murray didn't know what he could say. He wanted to say he loved Janochek. He didn't know him, really, but Janochek was the only adult who had ever looked at Murray and treated him like he mattered. Janochek knew Murray wanted to be in the cemetery, and he let him be there. Murray sank to his knees. "Oh, God, Mr. Janochek, I would never do that." He covered his face.

It was very still for a while. When Murray came back

from wherever he'd gone, he wondered if they had left. When he put his hands down, they were still standing there. Both of their faces were red. Murray stood up. Janochek was looking at him, and he lowered his eyes.

"Murray, I think a couple of my things may have gotten in your backpack by mistake."

"Oh, no, they didn't, Mr. Janochek. I've had it with me the whole day. I didn't take anything. I mean I didn't put anything in there. Just my lunch and some books."

"Would you show us?" Janochek turned to look at Pearl again. Still no expression on her face.

"Sure," Murray said. He would have done anything to get this over with. He went to the nearest headstone and picked up his pack, brought it over to Edwin, and set it down. He spread the top and pulled out his lunch . . . and right below it was another lunch.

Murray couldn't make sense of that. He had packed his books and his lunch that morning. He always threw the old bag away because any food left was probably rotten. He pulled out the other lunch. No, that was his lunch. He could feel how light it was because he never got a drink or a can of juice and he could feel the chips crunching. He looked back at the other bag he had just set down.

"I . . . I . . ." Murray was suddenly afraid to open the bags. He looked up to find Janochek watching him.

Janochek turned to his daughter. "Pearl, I think you can help us here, and I mean *right now*!"

Murray could see the lines in the back of Janochek's neck, and he could see Pearl's eyes get wider and wider. And then she took off running, back in the direction of the workshop.

Murray understood. Her revenge. This other sack.

Janochek watched her until she disappeared in the distance, obscured by foliage, and then turned back to him.

"Are both those your lunch?" he asked.

"No . . . no! I'm so sorry. I didn't do anything. I don't know what the other sack is. I don't know . . . ." Murray ran out of words.

He held his hand out and Murray gave him the bag that wasn't his lunch.

"Do you know what's in this bag?" Janochek asked, looking at Murray steadily.

"No, sir," Murray said.

"I think I do," Janochek said. "I'm very sorry for this. Please forgive my daughter and me for this upsetting intrusion."

Murray couldn't stop himself. "She's real mad at me."

Janochek hesitated and looked at Murray again. His face seemed weary this time.

"I know," he said. "I know." And then he walked away.

When he walked in with the sack, Pearl was sitting in the big chair, hands in her lap. He put the sack on his desk and pulled his swivel chair over near her and sat down. He waited a moment before speaking.

"I've been mad at you before, but I don't think I have ever been ashamed of you. Until today."

He remained still and Pearl didn't look up.

He began again.

"I love you. You're the only child I have and the only one I want. I love you with every cell of my body and all of my soul. And I want you to start at the beginning and tell me everything about what happened today. Everything. You took my things, you lied, you did exactly what I asked you not to do . . . . You don't want to be this kind of person. You know where this kind of behavior leads. Hell, you've experienced it."

Pearl was quiet for a moment. Then she began telling him how she had gotten interested in the grave kid because he was so strange and that when she teased him and tried to get to know him, he had told her to leave him alone. And how mad that made her and how it really hurt her feelings because she had kind of thought she was doing him a favor. She went slowly, but she didn't stop until she admitted taking the things and putting the sack in the kid's backpack when he wasn't looking.

When she finished, she looked up. The color had gone out of her dad's face and he looked older. Or maybe just tired.

"You didn't kick him out, did you?" she asked.

He shook his head, no.

"Is he still here?"

"Probably." There was more silence.

"I know what you want me to do," she said.

Silence.

"I'll do it tomorrow after school," she said.

He nodded and got up to start dinner.

Even before he opened his eyes, Billup knew it was morning. He could hear cars on the thoroughfare two streets over. His mouth was dry, and his eyes were crusted together but not so sticky that he couldn't open them. *Shit!* He was in his recliner, still wearing the same clothes from the day before. He tried to summon some saliva while he retraced yesterday. He was at the cemetery. He left there and drove to the mission. He helped serve dinner to some homeless families, washed dishes . . . and then what?

He levered himself up and went to the bathroom. In the last three or four months, there were quite a few mornings when he awakened without any memory of the night before. He walked back into the living room and looked out the front window. His Chrysler was sitting in the driveway. *Yes!* So he had taken the department car back to headquarters and got his own and then . . . he stopped at the Tropicana because he saw a car in the parking lot that belonged to an attractive community service officer. He didn't see her at the bar, so he went up, sat and ordered his usual, a double and a beer, probably, waiting, thinking she might be in the restroom . . . And nothing after that. Did he stay there and drink till they cut him off?

He went into his small kitchen. There was a brown sack on the counter. He checked it. Empty. He looked around the kitchen but didn't spot anything. He walked back to the living room. Between his recliner and the wall, lying on its side, was an empty bottle. Popov vodka. A quart. So now he knew. When he left the bar, he bought some to go and drove home. End of story.

A better ending than a few weeks ago, when he woke up in the city car at the rodeo grounds by the river, with mud on his clothes and the car seat and the floor mats. Took him over an hour to clean everything up. Or last month, when he found the city car in his driveway with a bash and scratches in the right front fender as if he had hit a pole or a divider somewhere the night before. He had been able to explain away that dent and damage as a parking lot accident that probably happened when he was at a strip mall opening the day before. He told motor pool he didn't notice it at first and suspected it must have been a hit-and-run, no note or anything. He never mentioned the part about not returning the city car at the end of some of his shifts, and no one asked him about it.

He went into his bedroom, hampered his wrinkled clothes, and got ready to shower and shave for work. When he got to his car, thirty minutes later, he walked all around it. No scrapes. No blood. He must have made it home okay.

Gates began calling associates, friends, and family of the three main suspects, asking whether Rudy or John or Buell ever borrowed anyone's car. Buell appeared to stay at home nearly all the time, and drove only his brown Taurus. John's clients reported that his red Miata convertible was a kind of trademark and he was never without it. Rudy, on the other hand, had access to a multitude of cars through his family. Mostly he drove a white Nova with a 327, glasspacks, and oversize tires on chrome mags. When the Nova was being worked on, Rudy drove his uncle's "M-car," a BMW rocket.

Gates called every dealership and car rental agency to see whether any of the three had rented or gotten a loaner during the month of October. Nothing new, except about the M-car, and it had not been searched. Rudy's uncle gave permission.

A joint city and county team stripped it to the metal frame, including the trunk, then reassembled it. Traces of marijuana and cocaine were found, but not enough to bother with prosecution. Other than that, nothing. No hair, no fibers, no link to the girl.

Gates was left with his earlier nagging suspicion that the investigation had yet to turn up the perpetrator. After another trip to the overlook for some quiet reflection, he had his next idea. While the high school was still in session, before the holiday break, he decided he would stake out the school every day for a week between the hours of 5:00 and 7:00 in the evening. Maybe there was something obvious that everybody was missing.

Murray was sitting on the grass, trying to make some contact with James. He never said anything, and Murray was trying to figure him out. He had closed his eyes and become very still so he could picture James. He saw a hawk-faced, thin young man in a bloody uniform. He saw him wandering in the mud, a tattered barbed wire-fence behind him. His hands were dripping blood. And then Murray saw James on the ground. Dirt clods were raining down. His forehead and nose were still there, but his jaw and chin and part of his neck were missing. His eyes were open and he was staring at the clouds. Murray was thinking, "If you can't talk, just send me some thoughts and I'll get it. I'd like to know you."

Someone cleared their throat softly behind him and broke his concentration. Murray turned. It was Pearl. He wondered if he had been speaking out loud.

"I came to say I'm sorry," she said.

Behind her, the irregular shapes of tombstones reminded Murray of chess pieces.

"That was a mean thing I did. I was really pissed at you. You wouldn't tell me what you were doing and . . . and I got so mad. I'm not even sure why." Pearl scuffed the ground with the toe of her shoe.

Murray didn't know what to say.

"Well, anyway, I'm sorry, and I won't do anything like that again, so you can do whatever it is that you're doing and I won't bug you anymore. I promise. I told you I keep my word, and I do, so you're safe from now on."

They continued to look at each other, Pearl standing,

folding and unfolding a sleeve of her jean jacket as she talked. Murray, sitting cross-legged about six feet away, wondering what he should say. She started to turn away.

"Wait!" It was out of his mouth, a bird flying out of a cage. "Have you ever been scared about what's going to happen to you?" He didn't know where these words were going. "You could get me thrown out of here . . . and I can't . . . Wait just a second, please, and let me explain something."

He gathered himself. "They could take me out of my home and put me someplace. I mean, I don't really live there much, but they could lock me away in a"—*Don't say mental hospital!*—"They might think I'm . . . I mean, you might tell your dad and then the County lady would come. I don't have anyplace!"

How could he ever explain? *Shit!* "I've got to stay here!" He was too loud. Desperate. "These people need me!"

"I don't have a mother," Pearl said.

Murray was derailed. "What do you mean?" he was irritated by her interruption. How could he get her to see what it was like for him?

"She's dead." Pearl was looking right at him. "She didn't want me. She kept leaving home. She only stayed around at the last when she was dying of cancer."

Murray was struggling to assimilate this. He looked around. "Hold on, hold on! She's here?" he asked, gesturing toward the cemetery.

"Don't tell me to *hold on!*" Pearl yelled at him. "You're not the only one who's got problems. Who has things to tell. You're not the boss of me!" She was backing up, getting ready to leave again.

He felt like he was talking to a burning fuse. "I know," he said, placating, shifting the focus from himself to her. Searching her face. "I'm asking. Please. Slow down. Give me a second."

She put her hands on her hips, then let them drop. "She's cremated," Pearl said. "My dad wouldn't bury her here. He told me it would be too hard on him in the long run, so we sent her ashes back to her family in Tennessee."

Murray was embarrassed, but it did make him feel better that she had some real sadness in her life. Maybe she could understand him a little.

He began again. "Let me start over. Okay?"

She didn't nod. Stood. Waiting.

"I'm sorry about your mom. I didn't know." He paused. She hadn't moved. He went on. "You know what I do here. I talk to graves . . . but it's really not the graves I'm talking to."

He gauged her reaction. She was still listening.

"This is the part I didn't want to tell you . . . because it is really the most important thing to me. I thought if you didn't understand what I'm going to tell you, you might get me kicked out like you threatened. And I can't go. I love it here. I'm needed here. If I couldn't be here, I don't think I could be anywhere anymore." He knew he was rambling.

The whole place was quiet. He couldn't hear traffic or anything.

"You're talking to the dead people," she said.

His eyes welled.

"You're talking to the dead people and you didn't want to say it because you thought I'd think you were crazy and get my dad to make you leave."

He couldn't speak.

"Wow. That really is out there. I mean, I thought you . . . Wow."

She pushed her hair back to her neck. She was shaking her head, slightly, side to side. "Why?"

"Because I hear them. I hear them. They talk to me! Sometimes I can even see what they looked like when they were alive." *Shut up!* But he couldn't.

Murray didn't dare look at her. He had never planned to tell her the truth. He closed his eyes and rubbed his forehead with his fingertips.

She took a couple of steps forward and sat down beside him. "I won't tell on you," she said, "but I want to hear more."

Murray felt a quick urge to yell, "What good would it do!" He didn't. "Okay," he said, "uh, cross your heart," and that just seemed so damn hopelessly stupid. *What a weenie!*

But she did. And she kept looking right at him. And he started talking.

"I don't even remember when it started. It was probably sometime last spring. I had been fighting a lot with my mom. I don't want to talk about her. And I wasn't getting along very well with anybody at school . . . and I came over here one day to be by myself. I got curious about what it would be like to die when you were young. And I looked at the tombstones like this one," he said, pointing to

GEORGE ARTHUR DICKSON
GAVE EVERYTHING THERE IS TO GIVE

"And I guess, at one point, I was sitting, maybe resting

57

against a tombstone, and I got a really strong picture in my head. It was a woman actually, 'Elizabeth Chandler, Dearly Beloved.' I was seeing her the way she was before she died. Clear as day, like we were connected. And I began to know her story, why she died and all. I was *listening* to her voice! And she was grateful to have someone pay attention to her, and we started talking."

Murray looked over at her. Pearl was holding her chin in her hands, waiting for him to go on.

"Over time, I got to meet most of the young people buried here. I got to hear their stories. This may sound stupid to you, but I'm like a friend to these people. I'm a guy who comforts them, and they appreciate that. Everybody needs a friend."

"Tell me about them," she said.

Murray told her what he was beginning to learn about James and about Blessed and Edwin. He talked about Dearly—about the car accident, her clothes, and her love of wildflowers, but left out the part about the underwear.

Pearl took a deep breath. "Okay," she said, "keep bringing me up to date." She thought for a second. "And take me with you from time to time, like today."

Murray made a decision, too. "I'll do that. I'll introduce you to my friends. I don't think you'll be able to hear them . . . but always, *always* keep your promise. Don't tell anybody, not even your dad." He checked her one more time to see if she accepted his terms.

She kept looking at him straight on.

"I promise," she said.

Something good was happening for Robert and he knew it. Yesterday, his county case worker, Peggy Duheen, noticed it. She said he was looking great when he walked in for his appointment. She asked what was going on with him. He thought about telling her that he was feeling like he could concentrate better, was even starting to get some of his memory back, and he just a little bit suspected that it was because he was taking his meds, as prescribed, every day. He was keeping his log! And he had been for almost two weeks now.

A couple of days ago, he had gotten home after work and found himself remembering what he had bought for his mother's birthday: a two-foot-high Asian-looking vase from the Bargain Emporium. And he remembered where he had put it, by his 33 rpm record album cover collection under his bed. He looked, and sure enough, there it was!

He couldn't think of the last time he had felt so proud of himself. But he didn't tell his caseworker about the log or any of those things. He didn't want to get her hopes up, in case he blew it. He told her, instead, that he was making money at TacoBurger and that if he kept the job another two months, he'd get a raise, and if he stayed another six months, he'd qualify for benefits. He told her that he was exercising, taking long walks three or four times a week and that he felt like he was pretty healthy. He didn't mention the cigarettes or the candy-bar diet.

Ms. Duheen was very supportive. She had probably never seen him so upbeat, probably never heard him talk about any long-range planning. She asked him how his medication was doing. Robert said it was fine, seemed to be working okay. She leaned toward him slightly and breathed in, like she might be checking if his clothes were clean, but she didn't comment.

He wondered if she noticed that, during their fifteen minutes together, he had looked her in the eye a couple of times. He realized that he didn't feel like complaining about the people in his hotel or his coworkers one single time. She didn't ask him about his voices, maybe because he really was doing better and she didn't want to bring him down.

Today he had taken his morning meds when he woke up to pee around nine, yes, there was the notation, and he had had a pretty good day at work with nobody bugging him too bad. He almost felt like celebrating, like calling his mom or something. He decided he would check the lobby newspaper when he got back to the Sadler and see what movies were playing at the downtown theater. He hadn't been to a movie since he lived at the halfway house, and he had overheard his coworkers saying tickets were cheap if you got there in the afternoon. Maybe he'd go.

Or maybe he would start checking out these parked cars around the courthouse and see if anybody left his keys in the ignition. Go for a ride. Be a race-car driver. Dale somebody-or-other. That would be fun, too. He was doing good. Probably time to take it to the next level. He was looking inside a Mustang convertible when he noticed a security guard watching him from the courthouse steps. *Bastard.*

Robert continued back toward his hotel. He thought about buying a chain for his wallet. He was walking tough. Feeling strong. Anyone could see he was a street warrior.

When Billup went through the pressurized doors into the lobby of police headquarters, the duty officer behind the first desk said, "Fowler wants to see you." Billup didn't like his tone of voice.

"Now?"

"Now."

Not good. Never good. Billup wondered what had happened. He climbed the stairs to the second floor and went down the hall past individual cubicles to Fowler's office. Fowler saw him through the door glass and waved him in. He didn't get up and he didn't invite Billup to sit. *Shit!*

Fowler was wiry, nothing but bone and muscle, with an Adam's apple like a golf ball.

"Brenda said she ran into you at the Tropicana last night. Said you were blotto. She said you hit on her and wouldn't back off till she cracked you in the nuts."

Billup made an effort to keep his expression blank. If he had hit on Brenda, there would be plenty of witnesses. So if he denied it, Fowler would probably discipline him for lying *and* conduct unbecoming and would probably suspend him without pay, pending an internal investigation. Worse, it might come to light that he was in a blackout at the time, and where would that lead?

"Yeah, I guess I had a couple too many and got a little too friendly. I'm sorry about that. I'll go apologize to her right away."

"That's harassment, you dumb shit!"

Billup thought fast. "Oh no, sir, I was just a little loopy

and trying to have some fun. Hell, you know, we all get a little wild sometimes after work."

"*After work* won't mean crap if she files a suit."

"Uh . . . uh, let me go apologize to her right away and—and I'll assure her this will never happen again. And I'll remind her we used to be kind of buddies. We were both Cool April Nights parade monitors a couple of years ago."

"Don't go near her."

Billup was pulled up short.

"Don't . . . What? Why?"

"She doesn't want to see you is why. She's still deciding whether to file. Probably talking to the union today. I can't afford this on my watch, numbnuts. And it's not the only thing. I've got two reports on my desk about you bracing hookers and offering to trade favors."

"That's a lie."

"Two different reports, two months apart, and neither of them knew each other."

"That's bullshit. Trying to slip a collar. That's all that is."

Fowler stared him down, and then looked at the bale of papers strewn across his desk. He picked up a departmental form of some kind.

"You don't think you have to turn your car in every night?"

By the time Billup left the office, he was on two weeks' suspension. No pay, no badge, no service revolver, and no contact with any member of the department during the internal investigation. Before his reinstatement hearing, Billup was to meet with a departmental employee assistance person who would assess his drinking and make a report to Fowler.

Billup was fuming on the way to his car. Police work never should have been opened up to women. *Harass, my ass! I'll shoot that slut.*

The lobby of the Sadler House was spartan. There was a faded brown couch that faced the front sidewalk window. It was occupied, as usual, by an elderly man and woman who sat there and read the paper and napped through the daylight hours. Past the couch was another seating area with two large easy chairs, arms pitted with cigarette burns. Nobody there. At the rear of the lobby, near the elevator that never worked, was a pair of rickety card tables with wooden chairs, where residents often played checkers, spades, or dominoes. One guy was there today, reading a paper. Robert didn't recognize him. Must be new, he thought.

Robert went up to the desk. The day manager wasn't there, but the janitor was leaning on the counter looking at a magazine.

Robert stopped several feet away from the counter. "Got today's paper?"

Without taking his eyes off the page, the man lifted his right hand and pointed to the guy sitting at a back table. Robert stood for a minute, trying to make up his mind whether the custodian had actually heard and understood him and whether the pointing was the answer to his question. *Asshole.* He turned and walked toward the back. If the guy treated him like the janitor had, Robert knew he was going to get super mad, and then he wasn't sure what he would do.

The new guy was somewhere around Robert's own age. He was wearing a black stocking cap that covered most of his hair. What was showing was oily and dark. He had on an old Nike warm-up jacket, cargo pants, and dirty sneakers. As Robert got closer, he could see that the guy had acne that made his face rough and scabby, and he was frowning as if it hurt to decipher the newsprint. Robert stopped near the table and cleared his throat to get his attention.

The guy looked up. "Hiya," he said. "I'm Bruce. I just got here from Felton. What's your name?"

Robert knew Felton was one of the places where Butte and Sierra counties sometimes sent people when they no longer needed to be on a locked unit, but when they weren't ready yet to return to the community. He wondered why the guy spilled his news so quickly. Robert tried not to tell anyone anything about himself. Safer that way.

"What's your name?" the guy repeated.

"That today's paper?" Robert asked.

"Yeah. I was just looking at it, trying to see what's going on around here. I just got here. You live here?" he asked Robert.

The guy was friendly. Robert could feel that. But maybe he was just after something.

"Got the movie section?"

"Yeah."

"Can I see it?"

"Yeah. Going to a movie?"

"Maybe."

"Can I come? I like movies. Sometimes I watch movies for days."

"How come you were at Felton?"

"My family thinks I'm crazy. I get all these ideas and I get doing 'em and I get where I can't sleep or anything and

65

then they make me go to treatment and that's where I wound up last time."

Robert was familiar with that scenario. That's the way the system works. If you have great ideas or if you are being followed and people are trying to kill you, the system locks you up and tries to get rid of you. This guy, Bruce, reminded him of his pal Donny in Chico.

"So how come you're here?"

"My dad didn't want me back home. I don't think I can go home anymore."

Robert was also familiar with that. His mom tolerated him, but she really didn't want him staying anywhere near her home in Corning. She was embarrassed by him.

"Which movie you want to see?" Bruce asked, thumbing through the paper's sections.

"I don't know. I don't know if I want to go to one at all. I was just . . . I just wanted to look at what's on."

Bruce handed the Current Events section to Robert. "They're in there."

Robert opened the pages and saw the boxed listings. None of it meant anything to him. *Screw it!* He handed the paper back and started to walk away.

"How about *Speed Demon*?" Bruce asked him.

Robert wheeled. "What?" Was this guy making fun of him?

"*Speed Demon.*" Bruce was smiling. "It's about some guys who fix up these really great cars. Hondas, Caddies, Maximas. They make them super fast and race them and pull robberies, and there's supposed to be some really great chase scenes."

66

Oh.

Robert shrugged to get his muscles to relax. "Uh, I don't know. Maybe. I got to go." He turned again to head up the stairs to his room.

"What's your name?" Bruce called after him.

Robert stopped and looked back. Bruce was still smiling. Like a nice guy.

"Robert," he said. And then he was up the stairs.

When Murray got home after his heart-to-heart with Pearl, the door was locked and nobody answered. He climbed over the short wall by the garage and went around back. As usual, the back door to the garage was open. The lock plate had been busted for the past couple of years, since one of his mom's boyfriends got enraged when she wouldn't let him in because she was entertaining another man. The guy, Murray had no idea what his name was, jumped the side fence and kicked in the back door. He barged inside and got in a fist-fight, first with the new visitor, and then with Murray's mom when she started biting.

The whole thing freaked Murray, who had been reading in his bedroom. He was afraid to call 911, afraid all three would turn on him. Luckily, a neighbor called and both men were escorted out in handcuffs. That was just before the County woman came for a visit. She was with a sheriff, and she called herself a child protection worker. Murray had been afraid they were going to remove him from his home. Sure, his mom had some problems, but so did everybody, and Murray didn't want to live with anyone new. What if they didn't even like him? Just took him in for the money.

Murray was relieved to have the place to himself for a while. He put his pack in his room and went to the fridge. The top shelf held an open carton of orange juice. Smelled kind of sour. He put it back. He didn't pick up the bottles of diet cola—they never tasted right to him. Nor did he bother with the flavored coffee creamers his mother liked so much. On the shelves below sat jar after jar of pickles and olives and maraschino cherries. The bins were empty except for a wilted head of iceberg lettuce and an unopened bag of carrots. He tore the bag, shook out several carrots, and headed to his room for dinner.

The next morning, his mom's bedroom door was still closed, so he didn't know whether she had made it home. He didn't try to find out. When he was showered and dressed, he took the carrot bag, rolled it closed, and put it in his backpack for lunch. He left the house and headed off for another day at school.

Billup woke up in his car. Lying in the front seat. The windows were steamed, and the salty, tangy smell of urine was everywhere. He sat up. He was wet. He was in his driveway. He looked around to see if any neighbors were out in their yards. When he didn't see anyone, he pulled his keys out of the ignition, opened the car door, and hustled for his front porch.

Inside, he closed the door quickly and leaned against it, breathing heavily. *What the hell is the matter with me?*

Yesterday came back to him. The suspension. After that, he'd driven around by himself for a while and then gone to Shasta Lake to Delia's for a pick-me-up. After that . . . he couldn't recall. He knew he had to cut this shit out. He went to his bedroom, shed his clothes, and took a shower.

God, his head hurt. A beer would help. He checked the refrigerator. There were some sodas, but no beer. He decided he'd better mostly stay home until he got a tighter handle on his drinking. Stay away from the hard stuff. Just have a little beer today to get on an even keel, and then limit his drinking to beer and wine, at least till this suspension was over. He'd like to get back at that Brenda bitch. He would, too. But that would have to wait. Meanwhile, the next order of business was to lay in some beer and pick up a burger for lunch.

When he was dressed, he went out to his car and rolled down all the windows so it would air out. He took his pickup to the Liquor Barn. Once he was inside, looking at the rows of wooden wine cases, the aisles of high-proof spirits, the standing refrigerators stacked with beer, he realized this would be an ideal time to stock up. Especially since he was on a two-week vacation.

Gates parked in the front of the small teacher's lot by the metal and wood shops, where he could watch the entire street that ran through the middle of campus. He was right across the street from the gym. He had brought his own car so he wouldn't be so obvious. People would probably think he was a parent waiting for his kid to finish an activity.

The afternoon sky was mostly gray with fish-scale clouds that usually ushered in colder weather. A few gold leaves were left on the sycamores, the oaks were getting bare, but the juniper and spruce on both sides of the gym were deep green and motionless.

Gates loved this country. Not the heat! Not the heat, but the peaks, the foliage, the lakes, the icy black Sacramento River, which ran the length of the town. He scanned the tallest trees for nests and the utility poles for hawks that would perch and wait for a meal to emerge. Last weekend, he saw that an eagle had built a nest in a big orange industrial crane that was sitting in a field out by the freeway south of town. An eagle in a crane. Birds of a feather!

At 5:47, he saw the school bus driver, Nostrum, drive by, heading in the direction of his home. Gates jotted it down with an asterisk. Tomorrow he'd call the man's supervisor and check what time Nostrum had put on his time card. If the school was right about him padding his hours, maybe he left work earlier on the day Nikki disappeared and had time to set something up. Gates wondered about Nostrum. Was he dissatisfied, pent up? Had he seen an opportunity, been rebuffed, and hurt the Parker girl to keep her from talking?

Gates didn't think Nikki would have gotten into the car with him, but he wasn't going to rule anything out.

Gates stayed, listening to the radio and watching the road, until 7:00. He had made a note on a three-by-five card of every car license-plate number and every pedestrian passerby during that time. There hadn't been many, and nothing seemed in any way remarkable or unusual.

By Wednesday, Gates was reluctant to have the radio on. He was feeling tired, and he was concerned that he might space out listening and possibly miss something. After an hour or so, there had been nothing to miss, except some jays that screeched constantly while they patrolled the small stand of spruce to the left of the gym. They screeched and flapped and generally intimidated every robin and thrush that came to those branches to rest for a minute.

He logged the bus driver again, driving by after work a little before 6:00. The supervisor had told Gates that Nostrum had padded his time card by ten minutes yesterday, but it was too small an infraction to write up. Gates asked the supe not to mention his tracking. He wanted Nostrum unalarmed, doing business as usual. As Gates watched him drive by, he felt his hope and his interest in the man slide away. The guy was a lump. Gates didn't think Nostrum had the energy to do anything bigger than cheat on his time card, or had the acting ability to fool the investigating officers.

Shortly after, Gates noticed a boy walking up the hill toward the gym. Skinny kid. Looked a little too old for high school. Black ski jacket, dark jeans, motorcycle boots. The kid didn't seem to see Gates. He walked on past the gym and over the crest of the hill, and down toward Eighth. Gates made a mental bet with himself that the young man had lost his license to a DWI, was attending the county alcohol and drug program nearby on Pioneer Street, and was now walking home.

During the rest of the hour, Gates saw some cars he had logged yesterday—parents picking up their kids, nothing out of the ordinary. He began to have doubts that his surveillance of the kidnap area would pay off. Still, he was going to give it another two days.

By Thursday, Gates was using his whole bag of tools to stay alert. The log helped. He set his wristwatch timer to go off every two to three minutes to remind him to keep sharp. He now recognized the parent and staff automobiles and when to expect them. The chattering of the jays had fallen below his attention threshold. He was having trouble forcing himself to stay there. You'd have done this for your son, you can do this for Nikki, he was telling himself, like a mantra, when his peripheral vision picked up movement down the hill toward the right. He turned his head. That young man again.

Gates thought he had come from the east side of Pioneer Street, not the west end, where the drug program was located. The kid was passing in front of the gym and, by God, if it wasn't a little after 6:00 again. Gates didn't believe in that kind of coincidence. He got out of his car.

"Excuse me."

The kid had been watching Gates approach.

"Get away from me!" he told Gates, breathing fast, nostrils

74

flaring. He seemed to be fighting the urge to run.

Gates had his sheriff picture I.D. and badge in his left hand and he held that out for the young man's inspection.

"I'm not bothering anybody! I'm taking my medication!" The kid was actually yelling.

Gates recognized him now. He had seen him at County Mental Health on one of the days when it was his turn to be the sergeant at arms for the competency court. Gates took a step back and held out both hands to show the young man that he had no weapon.

"Easy. Easy . . . I am not going to hurt you in any way. I'm not going to touch you or bother you, but I do have to ask you a question."

Mr. Robert Barry Compton got a cynical look that said he had heard that before and he knew that government people would say anything they needed to.

"No way! No way. I'm just walking. I'm not doing a thing and you can't bother me."

The young man was having a very fearful reaction to being approached. Gates imagined that in the past, officers may have mistaken this kid's mental symptoms for resistence, may have rousted him pretty hard, may have lied to him so they could subdue him.

Gates took another step back and put his badge holder in his pocket. He put both hands up in a gesture of surrender.

"Please listen," he said, speaking a little more slowly, hoping to relieve some of the young man's anxiety. "I need your help. I sincerely need your help. That's all."

The young man was still breathing hard, but he no longer seemed ready to flee.

Gates thought about the best way to phrase his request. He did not want to upset this fragile truce.

"My name is Deputy Roman Gates. We've met before, down at the County. I am trying to find a person who's been missing for about six weeks, and I am asking everyone I can think of to help me find her."

"Her?"

"Yes. Her name is Nikki Parker, and she is a cheerleader here at this school."

"I don't know her."

"No. I didn't think you did. But you still might be able to help."

"How?"

"I think maybe she got into a car right about where we're standing."

Gates was acutely aware that he might, at this moment, be talking to the perpetrator. His senses were on full dial. Maybe the young man had something to hide.

Gates knew lawmen could treat people pretty rough if they happened to mistake mental symptoms for resistance or even drug use. He made an effort to relax himself and communicate a sense of safety.

The young man repeated, "I didn't do anything."

Gates reassured him. "I know you didn't. I just need your help. Just for a minute. You'd be willing to help a missing person, wouldn't you? Help a person so they wouldn't get hurt?"

The young man remained very wary, but his breathing was slowing by degrees.

"Just take a second and help me figure something out. Just a second."

The kid waited.

"Do you take this walk every day?" Gates asked.

"No."

"How often?"

"Whenever I don't work. I got to go."

"Please, just a second to try and help this girl."

The young man held his position.

"So, you come by here, how often? Every couple of days or so?"

A barely perceptible nod.

"For the past few weeks?"

Again a nod.

"Okay. This is the really important part. About a month ago, did you maybe see a school cheerleader in a white-and-blue uniform come out those gym doors and get in a car? Or walk a little bit and then get in a car that pulled up in the street? Or maybe get pushed into a van? Did you ever see anything like that a month or so ago? It's really, really important."

The young man seemed to drift off when Gates mentioned a car. His face showed strain. He looked like he was making an effort to think, trying to remember something.

"A car. A cheerleader and a car. A car . . ." The young man didn't appear to be aware he was speaking. Gates watched the fellow struggle, but in the end, he looked defeated. Gates felt sad for the kid and disappointed for himself. Still, Gates knew from past experience that he could be fooled.

"I don't know," the young man said.

"You don't remember?" Gates attempted to clarify.

Gates could see that this question triggered annoyance

in the young man. He had expected fear. Gates couldn't read this person. At one level, he seemed too socially awkward to approach anyone on his own, unless he had to. On another level, he seemed unpredictable and quick to anger.

"Look," Gates said, in what he hoped was his most engaging voice, "I know that today you're just kicking back and getting a little exercise. I don't want to bother you any further right now. Why don't you think about what I've asked you, and I'll look you up tomorrow and see if anything came to mind."

"I work tomorrow."

"Where?"

"TacoBurger, but you can't come there." The man grimaced.

"Oh, don't worry. I wouldn't want to interfere with your work in any way." Gates quickly took out his pen and a note card and asked, "Tell me your name and where you live, and I'll come by and visit sometime tomorrow after you're done working. Buy you a donut or a cup of coffee or some cigarettes and see what you've remembered."

The man was looking past Gates, as if seeking an escape route. "No! No. You can't do that."

Roman was very calm and reassuring. "I have to. I have to help this girl. You don't want anything to happen to her, do you?"

Gates got the name: Robert Barry Compton. Gates got the hotel: the Sadler House. The young man appeared to grow more agitated with each question. When Gates told him that was all, Compton sighed audibly and part of the frown left his face.

"Is there anything else you want to add before you go?" Gates asked him, putting his pen back in his shirt pocket.

Robert hesitated, then said, "Mister."

"Mister?" Gates was confused.

"*Mister* Robert Barry Compton," Robert said.

"Oh. Oh, yeah, sure. Well, okay, Mr. Compton, see you tomorrow."

Robert walked on past him without further acknowledgment.

Gates was energized as he pulled away from the parking lot. He tailed Compton from a distance while he used his cell phone to call the dispatcher and ask for juvenile sheets and arrest records on a Compton, Robert Barry.

She called back shortly. Twenty-two-year-old Caucasian male. Born: Red Bluff. Juvenile had two arrests for drunk and disorderly and one for selling crank to fellow students at Corning High. Disorderly charges dismissed for time served. No fines. Compton pleaded guilty to selling and was assigned six months' community service. Judge tagged the record with a stipulation stating next offense was to be prosecuted as an adult. As an adult, one "resisting" in Chico last year, dropped to misdemeanor "disturbing," and then dropped altogether when Compton was remanded to the local psychiatric hospital.

That fit with Gates's final impression of Compton as walking wounded, not dangerous unless pushed into a confrontation. Still, Gates followed him to the hotel and checked by phone to make sure Compton was registered under his own name. He was going to keep close tabs on Mr. Compton. Gates thought Compton had become some sort of victim himself. But Gates believed that, if he could establish a little bit of a relationship, there was a fifty-fifty chance that he would learn something. Had Mr. Robert Barry Compton been returning to the scene of his crime?

CONFIDENTIALITY

The following morning, Gates's first assignment was to measure and photograph the latest vandalism at the county's new softball stadium: "jay loves doris" spray-painted three times around the ticket booth. Jay had been pretty busy, six prior incidents of the same message in the past two weeks. Later in the day, Gates would triangulate the incidents and see whether he could establish the probable neighborhood of Jay's residence. Plus, how many couples of Jay and Doris could there be in a town of ninety thousand? He'd nail this jerkoff before Christmas.

Afterward, he parked the patrol car in the front lot at Mental Health. At the reception desk, he asked when he might speak briefly with Peggy Duheen. The staff person recognized him by his face and uniform and said she would call Peggy.

A minute later, Peggy rounded a corner down the hall and headed toward him, smiling, her long strides rapidly diminishing the distance between them. As she got nearer, he saw she was wearing tweedy black slacks with a short fitted jacket of the same material. Her low-heeled shoes were a dark red that matched the shiny turtleneck under the jacket. How do women do it? Gates wondered. He tried to think if he had ever seen a shoe store selling matching tops.

"Roman Gates! Good to see you. What brings you out here? It's not court day, is it? Am I having a senior moment?"

"Hi, Peggy. No. You know I just can't stay away from these halls."

"Be careful. Talk like that might get you admitted."

They both smiled.

"Actually, I'm following some leads on an investigation and I need a thumbnail on someone I've encountered."

"So they finally caught me?"

"No, for once, it's not your criminal activity." Gates enjoyed their banter, passing the time on those long competency-review court days, when they sometimes stood in the hall together for hours.

"It's someone you work with."

"Staff?"

"No. He's early twenties, kind of stringy blondish hair, all the same length, but above his neck. Dresses like a street kid, black jeans, white tee, Doc Marten–type boots. Nervous eyes."

"I think I might know who you mean."

"Yeah, I've seen him going in your office before."

"Roman, if he's a client of mine, I can't talk to you about him like this."

"Peggy, I know. Believe me, I wouldn't want you to bend any ethics or divulge anything confidential. He's shown up a couple of times in the last week, and I just want a general picture, that's all."

"Roman Gates! I thought you liked me, and here you are, trying to get me fired."

"Well, Peggy, I apologize. This investigation is more than just work to me or I wouldn't ask. Can you help me in any way?"

"We have a Mental Health Forensic Task Force that meets weekly to share information on our clients with the police, Public Health, and the sheriff. Really to advocate for them. We see if they're in trouble, and see if we can handle it through mental health services, rather than through criminal justice. If that's appropriate."

"Who's the sheriff's rep?"

"Randy Henderson."

"Oh, yeah."

"You tell him you want to put whoever it is on the agenda for this Wednesday and ask to attend. We each sign a Memorandum of Understanding regarding interagency cooperation and confidentiality, and you get your information."

"So, I ask Henderson today, and the kid gets put on tomorrow's agenda?"

"Pretty sure . . . if you get him to request it before 4:00 today."

"It's a deal. Peggy, thanks a lot. I owe you."

"Well," she said, "traveler's checks, gemstones, or expensive cars are a good way to convey gratitude. Hey, I'll see you tomorrow." She turned and was gone while Gates searched for a reply.

As Gates walked back to his car, he was thinking how much he liked and respected Peggy Duheen. She worked in a tough business, like he did, and she managed to keep her warmth and humor. And she was always professional. He thought she was a little younger than he, probably early forties. He knew she had been divorced for a few years, but he didn't know if she was seeing anybody. She was sturdy and athletic and tall, maybe five foot ten, and she looked like she might be able to outrun him if she wanted to.

Maybe he could settle up by taking her to dinner someday. He got in the squad car and radioed the dispatcher to put him through to Henderson.

Robert had walked faster than usual back to the hotel, upset by the confrontation with the lawman. In his experience, nothing good ever came of encounters with the law. When he entered the lobby, he saw the new guy, Bruce, sitting at a rear table. He was playing cards with three other residents: two potheads with long, greasy hair, and a broken-down old man who was dying of something where he couldn't get his breath anymore.

Bruce looked up and said, "Hi, Robert," when Robert passed by on the way to the stairs. The pothead wearing the stained baseball cap looked up but didn't speak. Robert acknowledged Bruce with his eyes but didn't say anything.

Up in his room, he checked to see if he had taken his afternoon meds. Yes. And then he thought about the man. The man wanted to know about a car.

Robert pulled out his wallet and took out his Social Security card. That was the word he had written on it: *car*. Robert tried some of the tricks he had taught himself to bring back his memories. Rhyming: *car, bar, tar* . . . Picturing in his mind's eye all the different automobile brands he knew.

And then he remembered the guy asking about the cheerleader. The white-and-blue uniform. White car? White car, white outfit? Was that it? What had caused him to vow to tell somebody? What kind of car? There was something different about the car. What was it? And something else. Robert could feel it. Something else. Was it the girl?

Robert just couldn't bring it back into focus.

Gates arrived at Mental Health twenty minutes before the meeting started at nine. He found Peggy and they chatted in the hall in front of the admin conference room. Henderson was the next to arrive, a compact ex–steer wrestler. His handlebar mustache and black ostrich cowboy boots punctuated both ends of his sheriff's uniform.

"Gates. Glad to see you're finally here at Mental Health where you belong." He smiled. "Compton, huh?"

They were interrupted by a woman Gates hadn't met, wearing a Public Health identicard, and then by a guy in a sport coat who turned out to be the therapist manager of outpatient services. He opened the door to the room and everyone filed inside. Before they had chosen their seats, they were joined by a young Hispanic woman, who turned out to be the psychiatrist. And then, shortly, RPD's Officer Webber lumbered in, following his eighty-pound belly, and sat on the couch with a prolonged sigh that made Gates wonder if the man would be able to get up when the meeting ended. Henderson, at the other end of the couch, patted Webber on the knee.

"Always glad to see Riverton Police's finest."

Webber scowled at him. "Haven't they fired you yet?"

The psychiatrist introduced herself as Dr. Mendoza and suggested they get started. The outpatient services manager passed a clipboard that held the joint-department Memorandum of Understanding, which each person present had to sign, and then picked up the chart on the top of a rolling cart and read the name.

"Compton, Robert Barry."

Gates told the team that, when he had met him yesterday, Compton seemed very uncomfortable and suspicious, even somewhat volatile. He was hoping for suggestions about how to question Mr. Compton and elicit information about a current investigation without overly raising Compton's anxiety or triggering his anger. Further, Gates wondered if anyone on the team thought Compton might be capable of hurting someone in a crime of violence.

As Gates spoke, the manager opened the chart and thumbed through different sections of it. He summarized, "Axis I Primary Diagnosis: Schizophrenia, paranoid type. Etiology probably crank abuse. No family history of major mental illness. Secondary Diagnosis: Methamphetamine dependence, in remission.

"Dr. Mendoza, have you worked with Mr. Compton?" he finished.

"I have probably prescribed his medication. What is it?"

"Sorry. Uh, Risperdal, two milligrams *p-o, b-i-d.*"

"*P-o, b-i-d?*" Gates asked.

"Taken by mouth, twice daily."

"And the level of dosage?" Gates asked.

"Moderate," the doctor answered.

"Did I prescribe?" the doctor asked the manager.

The manager checked the record. "Yes, looks like you've seen him once in the last six months."

"I don't remember him. What does he look like?"

Peggy described Robert, ending with, "He's usually avoidant, wary, suspicious."

"I don't remember him. I see so many like that."

"I know," Peggy said. "Well, am I the only one who's worked with him regularly?" she asked.

No one spoke.

"He's been staying at the Sadler House since he came here from Chico about six months ago," Peggy said. "His Chico psych halfway house contacted us prior to the move, to arrange this placement. Robert started hearing voices as a young crankster in high school. He's one of the ones who was just loosely enough put together in the first place that, when he got crazy behind the crank, he never fully came out of it and remains paranoid, hearing voices to this day. He doesn't have the social tools to get much support from other people. He's a loner." Duheen had closed her eyes, remembering.

"Last week during our meeting, he seemed better than I've seen him before," she continued. "Who knows? If he stayed away from street drugs and took his medication as prescribed, he could pull out of it at some point and have a better life. I don't see him being violent unless he was cornered by someone he feared, or unless his full-blown paranoia returned, like if he stopped his meds or was using again."

"I agree," Dr. Mendoza added. "Sober, no more likely to be violent than the average person. More irritable, possibly. More dangerous? Probably not."

Gates broke in, concerned about the young man as a suspect. "Could he be using, not regularly, but once in a while? Or back to drinking like he did earlier and getting into blackouts where he's capable of who knows what?"

Dr. Mendoza thought this over. "Has he been deteriorating, staying at baseline, or improving over the last two months?" she asked Peggy.

"Actually, I'd say he's been stabilizing, getting some cognitive gains, and able to keep his job."

"Then it's a high probability that he's not chipping," Dr. Mendoza said. "If he were occasionally using crank, for example, once a week, say, his medication would be failing to hold him because of the huge neurotransmitter disruption that methamphetamine creates. We would be seeing deterioration.

"As for blackouts, any of us has the capability to do anything if we're that drunk. In a blackout, there will be no memory of an event or behavior. A person's executive functions become anesthetized. You probably know better than I that our prison system is filled with people who have committed heinous crimes in a blackout."

Gates realized that might explain why so many convicts adamantly claimed their innocence; they didn't remember doing the deed! Gates broke in before Mendoza could continue. "Executive functions?" he asked.

"When you take a drink, alcohol gets in your bloodstream, and begins to saturate your brain from the top, the cortex, down," she explained. "The first things to numb out are the executive functions: your ability to control your impulses and to consider the consequences of your behavior. You get bolder, less inhibited, more opinionated, more self-absorbed, less aware of your effect on others. Continue drinking and the numbing reaches lower in the brain. Gradually, centers like speech and balance become impaired. You slur, have trouble walking. You can drink so much you pass out and the anesthetization may reach the life-sustaining centers. Your breathing stops, or you vomit but don't wake to clear your airway and you drown in it. I'm sure you've come across deaths due to acute alcohol poisoning in your work."

As Mendoza talked, Gates was flooded with memories of deaths he had encountered. And then he thought about his son. He forced himself to refocus on what she was saying.

"It's unlikely that Compton's neurological balance could sustain even one big party without it being noticeable to Peggy in their sessions."

"Okay," Gates said. "So, what's the best way for me to approach him?"

Mendoza responded first. "Low-key. No pressure. Nonthreatening. Laid-back body posture. No quick gestures or movements. Give him plenty of physical space; don't crowd him. Introduce yourself and your purpose. Show him respect."

"He says exercise makes him feel better. Walking," Peggy said. "He smokes. He probably likes cars, even though he doesn't drive that I know of. Likes sweets. Any of those things might be an entry."

"Could you come with me to interview him?" Gates asked Peggy.

Mendoza quashed that instantly. "That wouldn't be appropriate."

The room was quiet then.

After a few seconds, the manager spoke. "Anybody got anything else?" he asked.

No one said anything.

"Okay," he said. "Thanks for coming, Deputy," and that was that.

The day manager at the Sadler had a thin black goatee that he probably thought made him look distinguished, but Gates thought it made him seem shrewd, possibly untrustworthy.

"Why do you want to see Robert?" he asked, eyes fixed on Gates's service revolver.

"He's not in trouble, if that's what you mean. Is he here now?"

"Well, I can't say. He came in a while ago, but he could have left through the laundry, or even gone out the front without me seeing him."

Gates suppressed some irritation. "Would you phone his room?"

"The rooms don't have phones."

Gates thought he would probably get more assistance from a paper clip. "What is his room number?"

"Three-ten. Second or third door on your left after two sets of stairs."

Gates left without thanking the man.

Robert was very cautious about opening the door. He kept the chain on and leaned just far enough around the side to make sure it was Gates. Gates invited him to walk the three or four blocks to Winchell's for some donuts. Robert seemed wary, but tempted by the donuts.

When they got there, Robert seemed surprised to see a fellow in a stocking cap sitting at one of the metal sidewalk tables talking with a girl and a guy wearing big backpacks. The young man hailed him immediately.

"Robert! It's me, Bruce. Hey! Long time no see! Come

here and meet Jeannie and . . . what's your name? Tom? Tom!"

Robert waved him off.

Bruce persisted. "Robert! Come meet Jeannie!"

Gates was holding the glass entry door. Robert had stopped, unsure. Gates whispered, "Tell him you'll come meet her in a minute." Robert seemed grateful.

"I'll come meet her in a minute," he said, and quickly entered the donut shop.

"Man, I missed lunch. I'm really hungry," Gates told Robert as they approached the counter. "I think I'll get a dozen. We can sit over here by the window and have some and then take the rest home. What do you want, some coffee or some milk?" Robert was barely listening, lost among the donuts. Gates told the counterwoman to give them two coffees, two milks, and a dozen donuts.

"I want an old-fashioned chocolate and two old-fashioned glazed and an apple fritter. You pick the rest and I'll pay."

Robert was absorbed. He started right up where Gates left off. "Two of those strawberry ones . . . and what are those?"

"French crullers," the woman said.

"And two of those. And two cinnamon rolls . . ." He looked at Gates. "Is that all right?"

"Sure. Whatever you'd like."

"And two of those lumpy ones with the white frosting. And two of those ones he got first. And . . . and that's all," he said, winding down.

"Okay," Gates told the woman. "Could you bring all that over to the table by the window?"

Gates told Robert to go out and say hello to his friends and then to come inside, and their food would probably be ready by that time. Robert went out, stiff and uncomfortable. The guy who had called to him seemed energetic and friendly, and Gates thought Robert had loosened up a little by the time he came back. Donuts covered most of the table space. Robert looked from one to the other, giving each donut its due.

"They look good, don't they?" Gates said.

Robert nodded without taking his eyes off the donuts.

"Which one you going to start with?" Gates asked him. "You pick first."

Robert picked up a strawberry donut with pink icing.

"Good choice," Gates said. "I'm going to have one of these old-fashioneds."

After Robert had chosen a cruller for his second, Gates gave him time to chew, and then said, "So, tell me anything you feel like about our discussion a while ago. Have you remembered anything? A girl in a white-and-blue cheerleader outfit getting into a car about a month ago?"

Robert was reaching for a chocolate donut. He had been fairly relaxed, but when Gates said the word "remember," he drew back his arm and sat up straight.

"I can't remember things," he said, looking down and off to the side of the table.

Gates made himself relax and smile. "That's okay," he said. "We'll just sit here and eat, and I'll tell you what her cheerleading outfit looked like and you can just tell me anything you think of. Don't worry. Anything you say will be of help to me and will help her, because I wasn't there. I don't know anything about what happened, so I am going to appreciate everything you say. Whatever you say will help that girl." Gates made himself sit back and pick up one of the donuts.

"She was sixteen years old and she had"—*past tense!*—"she has brown hair down to her shoulders and her name is Nikki, and that day she was wearing—"

"A white outfit," Robert finished for him.

Gates felt a surge. "Yes, a white outfit. Did you see it?"

"No. You told me."

Gates smoothed himself out again.

"Yes, you're right. A white outfit with a blue letter on the front. And her skirt was pretty short and it was the same color, white, and it was lined in shiny blue material that sometimes showed when she walked."

"I didn't see her walk."

Gates stayed within himself. "You didn't?"

"No." Robert was spaced out, eating another donut. "She was in a car."

"In a car."

"She was . . ." Robert looked up at Gates and seemed to reorient himself. "I don't remember," he said.

"I love cars," Gates said.

"Yeah."

"What kind of car do you think she was sitting in?" Gates asked, his voice dead level.

Robert dropped his eyes and chose another donut. "Maybe a white car," he said. He looked up again. "Did you tell me that?"

"No, I don't think so," Gates said. "What kind of car could it have been?"

"What kind of car?" Robert repeated.

Gates was silent.

"A white car, maybe. With something different. With something different, I think. I tried to remember. I told myself to remember, but I couldn't."

"Gosh," Gates said, "there are lots of things that make cars different."

"Yeah."

"Was it an old car?"

"I don't think so."

"Was it an SUV?"

Robert shook his head, no.

"Was it all dented like it had been in a wreck?"

Again no.

"Was . . . was it all souped up? Uh, lots of chrome . . . mufflers rumbling?"

"Souped up?"

"Yeah, uh, tricked out, big engine. Oversized tires, mag wheels?"

"I don't think so."

"Did it have any sign on it?"

"I don't know."

"Well, what else could make a car different?"

Robert scanned the donuts and chose the other strawberry.

"Spotlights?" Gates asked.

"What are those?"

"Never mind. Big loud bass speakers?"

"I don't think so."

Gates gave up. This was a start. Maybe Compton saw

her in a car. Maybe the car was white. Nikki's ex, Rudy, had a white Nova. Maybe more would come to Compton the more comfortable he got. Compton's memory seemed to improve when he was contented and a little distracted.

"You like steak?" he asked Robert.

"Are you a queer?" Robert asked.

"No," Gates said, surprised. A funny question at this moment. "Why?"

"What's in it for you?" Robert said, holding another donut.

"I want to help the girl," Gates said. "And I don't know anything. And you do know some things, even though it's not easy for you to remember. So I think you're a good person who wants to help this poor girl, and I want to assist you in any way I can to recall the things you saw happen."

"Oh," Robert said, losing interest. "Can I take the rest of the donuts with me?"

"Sure," Gates said, smiling. "Eat them all yourself or give some to your friends, whatever you want."

"Okay."

It was a warm December afternoon and they walked back to the hotel without saying another word.

Murray was sitting with Dearly.

"She's spunky," Dearly said.

"Yeah, she is. She's also a pain in the butt, but she grows on you."

"Can she hear us, too?"

"No. I just tell her what you look like and what you say. So far, she's interested, but I don't think it will last long. I think she was just curious and probably wanted a little something to do around this place."

"Does she help her father?"

"Not that I've seen. She plays basketball and does homework and reads and stuff."

"So maybe she's kind of bored? I think I would have been."

"Are you bored now?"

"No. I don't know how to explain it. There's nothing. And then there's you. Like those frogs in the desert, and then there's rain, and they come to life, and then it dries up and they're gone again."

Murray didn't know what to say to that.

He changed the subject.

"So, have you heard any new voices or anything unusual yet?"

"No. You still don't know what that voice is about, huh?"

"Nope."

"Why don't you check it out with Pearl? If she's a little bored, she'd like a good riddle."

Murray walked over to run that by Blessed. She was in

a good mood since he'd brought Pearl by, and he was interested in her take on bringing Pearl into the puzzle. Blessed had given him good advice in the past.

"Hey, Punk Nasty, what's cooking?"

Yeah, they were back on old terms.

"Hi, Blessed." He could see she was smiling. "Have you heard anything more about a new person in here?"

"Nope. This is a whole city. We don't really need any new people."

"Right, people are going to stop dying because you don't want to be overpopulated."

"What's up?" Blessed often seemed to know what Murray thought before he did.

"Well, about this new voice I think I've been hearing . . . Dearly thinks I should let Pearl in on the idea and see what she comes up with. I mean, I think that's kind of silly, because she doesn't even hear you all, so how could she help?"

"Hmm. Interesting. Well, Pearl's a pretty sharp cookie. She reminds me a little of me. She's smart. And she's determined. And she's mobile. And she knows this cemetery as well or better than you do. Why not?"

Yeah, he thought. Why not?

Robert was chopping lettuce, a job that drove him nuts. He hated lettuce. It didn't do any good. It just took up space. It didn't have any nutritions or anything. He had learned that at school. Plus, when you were chopping the stuff, you had to pay attention or you might lose a finger. What a freaking rip-off. Lose a finger to some goddamn lettuce. Stupid job.

He finished, and the dippy do-right came over and gave him tomatoes.

"Chop 'em, don't slice 'em. They're for the taco bins."

Robert hated his boss guy. The kid was younger than Robert, wore stupid wire-rim glasses like he was smart, and had the kind of superior attitude that made Robert feel murderous. He knew he better get his mind on the tomatoes before he did something dumb. He chopped as quickly as he could—a sloppy job really, but he was the one who put the crap on the tacos, so who was going to know?

When he finished, it was time to fry up some more chalupa shells. Robert was putting them in the basket and the basket in the hot oil when the noise of an argument caught his attention. He looked around. Nobody arguing in the restaurant. He looked through the take-out window. There it was. A guy and a girl yelling so loud it was coming over the orders speaker.

". . . your goddamn dog out of the front seat and shut your hole, you scuzzy bitch, trailer—"

"—the cops, you junkie bastard. You hit that dog again and I'll cut . . ."

And Robert zoned out because he had another piece. He had another part of the memory.

"Compton, I swear to God! Take the chalupas out before they're black, and watch what the hell you're doing! Wake up! I can't keep telling you . . ."

Robert did what he was told. He was on automatic pilot. His hands and body were setting the chalupa basket on the drain board and picking up the tortilla rack to make another batch of taco shells, but his mind was stopped on the street in front of the gym.

They were arguing. The guy and the girl were fighting! And he hit her. Right in the neck. And she shut up. And the guy drove off, looking at the girl, and never even saw Robert. That's what Robert had wanted to tell somebody!

Was the girl wearing a white outfit? Robert couldn't remember. But he did the one new thing he was learning to do. He got out his wallet and pulled out his Social Security card and wrote "argu."

Now he'd have something to tell that guy when they went out tonight to the wherever it was for steak. Steak. Robert remembered that.

Pearl caught up with him later in the day when he was talking with Edwin. Edwin was asking Murray how come he didn't want to drive.

"I always wanted to drive," Edwin said, "since I was six or seven, playing trucks in my sandbox. My dad used to put me on his lap and let me steer when we were alone in the car, driving to the grocery store or someplace. It was great."

Nobody had ever shown Murray anything. Nobody except teachers. He thought back. His mom had shown him how to fix breakfast cereal and how to boil eggs and how to wipe his butt cleaner so kids wouldn't tease him and call him "Stinky." But drive?

Pearl touched him on the shoulder, breaking his connection. Why did he *never* hear her coming?

"Hi. How did you get to be so quiet when you walk?" Murray asked her.

"I don't know. You learn more that way. What are you doing? How's what's-his-name?" She looked at the stone. "Edwin."

"He's pretty good. We were just talking. Hey, I got something I want to ask you. Dearly and Blessed thought maybe you could help me figure something out."

Murray told her about the new voice he had heard, and how it seemed different from the others. And how, if he was hearing it right at all, it seemed like it was lost or distressed, and he couldn't locate it.

"Tell me again what it says?"

"Well, I think it says 'him me' or 'hid me.' And 'fine' or

'find me,' and 'plea.' Maybe more, but I can't understand it. That's all I can get so far."

"Do you get any picture?" she asked.

Right then, Murray realized that Pearl was really into this whole thing with him. She wasn't questioning or judging everything he said. She was imagining in her own mind right along with him. Like a friend would. *Sweet!*

"No. Everything is fuzzy, like a TV without the antenna hooked up."

"Huh." She sat down beside him. "So, tell me again, where do you hear it?"

"Where your dad is putting most of the new people."

"The front third or so, nearest the street."

"Yeah."

"Okay." She was twisting the ends of her hair and staring right through him. "Okay, let's take one thing at a time. If the voice said 'hid me' and 'find me,' where would you hide someone in a cemetery?"

Good question.

"Uh, in the lawnmower shed."

She gave him a withering glance. "My dad is in there every day and checks the lock on his rounds."

"Uh, in a crypt . . . or in that big stone building——"

"The columbarium!"

They jogged to the big tan stucco columbarium, which had always looked to Murray like a small bank building. The front was marble, divided into orderly rows of compartments. Most had paper or plastic bouquets stuck through the door latches. Murray and Pearl pulled on every handle, but each was locked tight. If they couldn't open them, they couldn't see how anyone else could, either, without wrecking something. When they were done, Murray was shaking a little bit, but he didn't let her see it. What if one had pulled open and a body had rolled out?

"Crypts," she said. "How many are there?"

"I don't know. I'm not sure. I've never been in one. I never really thought about it."

"You've never been inside one? What kind of spook chaser are you?"

Murray looked at her. They both laughed.

"Have *you* ever been inside one?" he asked her.

She shook her head, no.

"What kind of cemetery brat are you?"

It felt good to let off a little steam.

"What about the crypt with the stone angels on top, over by Edwin's?"

"Yeah," she said, "let's check it! And there's the one just beyond the workshop, with the big statue of that woman with a scarf over her head."

Pearl and Murray went to the angels crypt near Edwin first. Murray had never looked closely at a crypt before. Had never touched one. Crypts looked like miniature ancient temples, cold and windowless, with a front door you could bring the coffins through. Murray held back. This one was beautiful but creepy. Pearl marched right up and tried the door. It was locked and jammed so tight she couldn't even move it.

After that, they tried the Mary Magdalene beyond the workshop. They could jiggle the door some, but the whole thing was chained shut with a substantial padlock. They walked to the end of the cemetery property high on the main road and checked for crypts they could see from there. By dusk, they had spotted four and tried them all, and they couldn't get into any. None of the doors looked damaged or disturbed.

They agreed Pearl needed to ask her dad if they, or she, could go inside each one. Murray had to ask her, what if her dad wanted to know why?

"I told my dad a few days ago that I was writing a paper on cemeteries. I'll ask him if I can see what crypts look like. I'll tell him you and I have been getting along better, and I'll ask him if you can come, too."

That would work. In fact, it was brilliant. That would even explain what they were doing if he saw them messing around the cemetery together. Research!

Murray had always been curious about the crypts. Most of them were decaying and neglected but beautiful. They were old, stucco over cement or bricks, he thought. At least the first two they had seen today were. The exteriors were weathered a dark gray, mottled and water stained, with splotches of green lichen and ochre-colored mold making random designs on the sides. The doors were usually iron, a little rusty but still strong. Near the top of the door, thin bars, like a grate, would let in ventilation. They reminded him of old monster movies.

"I'll ask him tonight," Pearl said, "and I'll see you tomorrow after school."

They said good night. Murray was excited and that was new, and it felt great! He walked around for the next hour, asking his friends the hide-a-body question.

"I'd try to stick them in one of the crypt houses, I guess," Edwin said.

"And if not there?"

"In one of the bushy areas, probably. It gets pretty dense. When the plants are close and the branches are low, you can't really see inside. You know where it would be really neat to hide? I read this in a book."

"Where?" Murray asked, glad that Edwin was taking the question seriously.

"In a tree. This kid hid on a high limb and bad guys were searching all over for him, but they never looked up!"

Blessed wasn't as much help. "I wouldn't hide anybody in a cemetery. I really wouldn't. I think they're a little creepy."

"Yeah," Murray said, "but say you did."

"Gee, I don't know. In the girl's bathroom? No guy would ever look there."

Not an idea really worthy of Blessed's intelligence.

Dearly was supportive, as always. "Let's see," she said, considering. "Maybe I'd try to put her in plain sight. Some place so obvious she'd be overlooked. A while before I died, there was a movie called the *House of Wax*. Ever hear of it?"

"Yeah, that mean-looking Vincent Price guy, right? My mom let me rent dozens of those old horror movies when I would stay home sick," he said, remembering.

"Yes, well, didn't he cover people in wax and display them so nobody would know he had murdered them? Museum visitors saw them, but they didn't realize what they were looking at."

"So how would that work here?" Murray wondered.

"I don't know. Plaster somebody and stick them in front of those little houses? Or whatever. The main thing is that if you two keep working on this, you'll figure it out."

Janochek was surprised that Pearl didn't complain about another night of ham sandwiches and coleslaw. Even though he suspected that Pearl actually loved ham and coleslaw, she always griped about having them so often. Last week, she had used a new vocabulary word to describe their dinner: *swill*. They had both laughed. When he asked her what the word meant, she didn't know. She had heard it during lunch at school, she said, and the other kids laughed, so she did too.

She also surprised him in the middle of dinner by bringing up her paper on the history of cemeteries. He had thought that was just a ruse to distract him and keep him from asking questions about whether she had plans to take revenge on Kiefer.

"So, I'm to the part where I need to describe some of the different kinds of burial places. And I realized I've seen the outside of the columbarium but don't really know what the individual lockers look like. And I've never even seen inside a crypt. Do you have the keys to any of the crypts here?"

Janochek smelled a rodent. He hadn't seen her writing any long assignment during the past week. She had never been particularly interested in his work. He put his sandwich down so he could watch her more closely while she talked.

"Do you? Because I would really be interested in seeing what they look like in there."

"I have the keys," Janochek stated noncommittally.

105

"You know what else?"

Janochek waited. Punch line, he thought.

"I've gotten to know that Kiefer boy a little better since I apologized."

Whoa! Janochek didn't like what he was suddenly thinking. Was Kiefer putting a move on his daughter? Did they want to get inside those little buildings so they could do God-knows-what in privacy?

"What?" Pearl must have caught him narrowing his eyes. "What?" she pushed.

Janochek chose his words carefully.

"I know I don't need to tell you that the safety and the sanctity of this cemetery are my responsibility, and I take that charge very, very seriously."

Now they were both examining each other minutely, seeking clues.

"I know that, Dad. I would never do anything to jeopardize your work here."

Janochek smiled in spite of himself. *Jeopardize.* Another new word.

Pearl marched on, apparently determined to reassure him, though she probably didn't suspect the exact nature of his unvoiced concern. "I just want to see what they look like inside, really, each and every one. I'm just curious. It'll make my writing better, and I know Murray would like to see, too. He spends so much time here, it's like a second home. He really cares about this place, you know. We're not going to do anything weird in there."

Murray. So that's how it's gotten. Janochek was not reassured.

"You would be with us, Dad. And you could lock up again after we looked. And we could do it at a time that wouldn't be an inconvenience. Whenever you say."

Could she actually be telling the truth? Janochek wondered. Was he projecting his own boyhood lust on the Kiefer kid? Janochek thought maybe he had become a little too cynical.

"Okay." He made a snap decision he hoped he wouldn't regret. "Okay, let's do it tomorrow. I'll finish my rounds early and we'll walk around before dark. I'll collect the keys and bring that big flashlight because they're pretty dark inside. There are about four or five of what they call garden crypts, and the columbarium. High groundwater's not a problem in this area, and people don't seem to mind going right in the ground. We should be able to see everything in around an hour or less."

"Thanks, Dad. I'll tell Murray. That will be really interesting."

Janochek continued to try and read Pearl's true motive in this project, but her face was impenetrable. His gut told him this was a ploy of some kind and that she was going to stall out her school-paper cover story as long as possible so he would forget to ask to read it when it was done.

"But here's the deal," he said. "I'll do this, but I want to read that paper as soon as it's finished. Cemetery history fascinates me, and I want to see what you say about it." He felt like he was trying to surround a queen with a couple of pawns. I'm out of my league, he thought.

When Robert got back from browsing Rite Aid after work, the first person he saw when he entered the lobby was the new guy. Bruce was standing near the front window by the divan, talking with an old man.

"Yo, Robert!" Bruce had spotted him. He quickly finished his conversation and was walking up, heading Robert off before he could reach the stairs.

"Hold up, hold up!" Bruce was closing fast. "I want to ask you something."

Robert hated being rushed up on. Was the guy going to run right into him, for crissake?

"Stop!" he yelled at Bruce. That was as loud as he could ever remember speaking. It was either that or hit the guy.

Bruce stopped and held up his hands like he was under arrest. "Take it easy. Take it easy. Cripes, man, I like you, but you are so sensitive. Chill, dude. I got something to tell you."

Robert tried to calm his breathing.

"*Speed Demon* is playing tomorrow afternoon at four, man. And it's on this side of town and it's cheap. Four bucks! Four bucks, and we can buy our own candy over here at that big store beforehand and not spend major bucks for that theater crap."

"Rite Aid."

"What?"

"Rite Aid. That's the store's name." Whenever Robert remembered a detail, it was important, a victory. He didn't know what else to say.

"Yeah," Bruce said, a little puzzled. "Okay, Rite Aid.

But, so, how about it? Let's go. It would be fun. Guys out on the town. Let's do it!"

Robert was stymied. He couldn't think of any reason not to, except that he was kind of afraid, and he didn't want to admit that to Bruce, or anybody else, for that matter. He had the money. He had been thinking about seeing a show.

"I can't tonight."

"I'm not asking about tonight," Bruce said. "Tomorrow afternoon. Tomorrow afternoon." Bruce acted like the repetition would filter through. He was making a visible effort to hang in there with Robert, trying not to seem too impatient.

Robert had given Bruce some thought. Bruce probably already knew that, in this hotel, Robert was about the only one working, about the only one who had any money to spend on nonessentials. And Robert knew that Bruce had some money, too. Yesterday Bruce had told him that, although his dad had thrown him out of the house, he still sent him a fairly generous monthly allowance.

Robert could tell Bruce thought he was slow, a little thick. Well, screw him, Robert thought. *Yeah, he's quick but I'm careful. You can't be too careful.*

"I'm going out for steak tonight." Robert wanted to establish some order here.

"Right. Right! That's very cool. Good for you. You going with the donut guy?"

Robert nodded.

"Great!" Bruce said. "That guy your dad or your uncle?"

Robert shook his head, no.

"Well, great," Bruce said. "Tonight, steak; tomorrow,

movie! Something to look forward to! See you then. Get some candy, walk to the movie. Three o'clock. Down here in the lobby. Don't be late. Takes about twenty minutes to walk over there." He headed off toward some people who had just come in.

Robert, unaware that he hadn't really made a decision, knew he needed to write this down, right away. *Tomorrow afternoon. Three o'clock. Here in the lobby. And today, steak.* He climbed the stairs, repeating it like a litany.

Waldrop's office was in a two-story wood-frame house two blocks east of the courthouse. Billup had been up since eight getting ready for this ten o'clock appointment. He was sitting in the waiting room, wondering if he had put on too much English Leather and how Waldrop would know he was there. At five minutes after ten, a woman opened one of the doors to the room and looked out.

"Mr. Billup? Come in, please."

Her office had one of those Persian-design rugs on top of another, larger rug. There were two chairs on either side of it, facing each other, and some kind of Far East artwork on the walls that Billup didn't care for. She sat in a substantial brown leather club chair and motioned him to a matching one across the rug. As he sat, Billup took her measure. Thirties, heavyset, round face, expensive-looking woman's suit with an annoyingly frilly blouse under, insincere smile. She picked up a file folder from the table next to her.

"So, Officer Billup, we're here today to discuss the relationship between your drinking and the pass you made at a fellow police officer."

Jesus, Billup thought, this broad doesn't beat around the bush.

"What relationship?"

"Officer, you and I both know it is very unlikely you would have so seriously offended this woman if you were sober. Moreover, the incident took place in a bar, where, at the time, witnesses state you had been drinking heavily."

"Look," he said, hoping to set this woman straight and

get this over with, "I was a little high and I got a little too friendly with a woman I thought I was pals with because we had worked together a lot."

"Twice."

"Okay, twice."

"You were friendly enough to get slapped with a harassment suit. She filed."

Shit!

"Officer Billup, thus far you have tried to minimize the gravity of this situation. I want to understand your perception of the groping incident, and what you think about your drinking problem."

Groping incident! Billup resisted the urge to throttle her.

"Sir, unless I am satisfied today that you are abusing but not yet addicted to alcohol—"

"I don't have a drinking problem!" Billup interrupted.

Waldrop ignored that. "Unless I believe that you understand your behavior well enough to modulate it, I am going to recommend continuing suspension and a mandatory alcohol/drug program. Are we clear?"

Ball-breaking bitch! "Yes, ma'am. I understand."

"Good. Now let's begin. How much do you drink?"

"Most days I have a beer or two, sometimes I go a little overboard. No more than anyone else in the department."

"Some people in the department don't drink."

Billup was surprised.

"Are you able to make a conscious effort to cut back your drinking when an occasion demands it?"

"Of course! I never drink at work." Billup didn't think there was a shred of evidence that he *had* on those afternoons.

"How do you feel talking about your drinking with me or with your supervisor?"

"It pisses me off because it's a false issue."

"Do you ever have a beer or a drink the day following heavy drinking, to settle your nerves or as an eye-opener in the morning?"

"No, no. If I should happen to drink too much one night, I don't want to see it again for days. Don't want to smell it. No, I'm careful."

"Why would you need to be careful?"

"Damn it! Don't interrogate me!" Billup heard his voice getting way too loud for the small room. He backed off. "Everybody's careful. Why wouldn't they be?" he asked, his voice back to normal volume.

Billup noticed that Waldrop pulled back when he yelled. Maybe she thought he might lose control. Crap, Billup thought. As if he would hit her or do anything funny when she practically had his life in her hands. He'd have to play the rest of this session real cool. He didn't want her to tell Fowler that he was a loose cannon.

"Officer Billup." Waldrop maintained her distance. "Let's move on to your family. Did either of your parents drink?"

Billup left her office feeling agitated. He didn't think it went well. He wished he hadn't raised his voice. Still, he felt relieved to have this over with, and his meeting with Fowler wasn't until the following Monday.

Now maybe he could enjoy the rest of his little vacation. He wondered how much better Costco's prices were than Liquor Barn's.

Driving to the Sadler House, Gates realized he had been looking forward to dinner with Robert, and not just because of the investigation. He admired the guy for working and not trying to milk the system. He could feel that Robert wanted to make it on his own.

He was going to let Robert decide where they ate tonight. He wanted him to feel as comfortable as possible, in control. Robert was down in the lobby, pacing, when Gates arrived. Gates checked his watch. He was five minutes early. He took it as a good sign that the young man was eager to see him, or maybe, he realized, just eager to get this over with.

When Robert got into the pickup, Gates asked him where he'd like to go for a steak. Robert gave him a blank look. Obviously, the question had not occurred to him.

"Any place you like?" Gates prompted.

"I don't know." Robert was facing forward, looking out the windshield.

"I know some good places," Gates said. "Shall I choose?"

"I got something to tell you," Robert said.

Gates did not show any reaction. "Well, great," he said. "How about we go to . . ." Now he wanted someplace near, before Robert forgot. He wanted to be able to watch Robert as he spoke, to gather every nonverbal cue he could.

"How about we go right over here to Bistro Rouge?"

Gates turned off the engine and they walked across the street. Bistro Rouge was quiet and expensive. He didn't think the boy had ever eaten there—probably had never even noticed the place.

"Get a steak?" Robert asked, making sure the deal still stood.

"Sure, get a big steak, baked potato or french fries, whatever you like, and you can fill me in on what you remembered."

Waiting for the salad to come, Robert seemed impatient to begin. He doesn't want to forget it, Gates thought.

"So," Gates said, "what did you recall?"

Robert told him about the argument that day at TacoBurger. He said that had made him remember he had seen a guy and a girl fighting even worse than that at the high school. They were in a car and the man hit her and she shut up and he drove away real fast.

Gates tried to recall if he had unintentionally planted any of this picture in the young man's mind. No. He had asked if Robert saw the girl walking and Robert had volunteered that she was in a car with a man.

"Do you think this girl was wearing a bright white cheerleading outfit?"

"Maybe."

Gates was having trouble concentrating. *The father!* Could it have been the father? He picked her up, they argued, he hit her, maybe accidentally killed her. Maybe she was going to expose him for molesting her.

Gates realized he didn't even know the girl's father. Hadn't seen any statements from him in the investigation reports. They hadn't searched *his* car! Robert had said "maybe a white car." Gates could hardly restrain his impulse to call the station and get the DMV report on the Parker family's cars.

The salad had arrived and Robert was chowing down. Gates picked at his, no longer hungry. When Robert finished his salad and mopped up the dressing, Gates spoke again.

"When you think about the man in the car with the girl, what did he look like? How old was he?"

This was important. Robert knew it. "Uh, the guy in the car was a guy, he wasn't a boy."

"You mean he was definitely older than the girl, not another student?" Gates bit his tongue. He must not supply his own ideas to this young man and taint the only eyewitness account he might ever get.

"Yeah, I don't know."

"What do you mean?"

"The guy was angry. . . . He was like you."

"In what ways? You mean he was a big guy? Brown hair? Wore a uniform?"

Robert thought about that. He could see the guy sitting in the car like on a distant TV. It was all of a piece and no detail presented itself. And then the steaks arrived and the picture faded.

While Robert began cutting his meat, Gates excused himself, saying he needed to use the bathroom but making a call to the station instead.

By the time the meal was finished and Robert had eaten his Chocolate Decadence and the rest of Gates's chocolate mousse, Gates was ready to try again.

"So they were sitting in a car at first. What was the car like?"

Robert struggled to re-form a picture of the scene.

Gates tried to set the stage without compromising the information. "So they were in a car near the front of the high school, and they were arguing and he hit her. How did you know they were arguing?"

"I could hear them yelling. That's how come I looked in the first place."

"So you looked and what did you see?"

Robert struggled to make the picture come to his mind. "A pretty big white car . . . and this guy and girl were yelling at each other in the front seat and . . . she was kinda pretty. She had brown hair. And his head was turned toward her and . . ."

"What was his hair like?"

"Like yours."

"In what way?"

"I only saw the back, I think, but it wasn't long."

"What color?"

"Brownish maybe. He had a big neck."

"What made you think so?"

"I don't know." Robert had a sense of the guy's power, the way he swung his arm so fast and hit the girl. Scary!

Gates didn't want to push any farther tonight and run the risk of driving Robert away. He had new information. Time to follow up on that and give the young man a break.

"Well, I'm full!" Gates put his hands on his stomach, but the truth was, he could barely remember eating. "How about we head home for the night and maybe get together in a couple of days. Maybe get an ice cream sundae. I know a good new place across town I think you'd like."

That sounded good to Robert.

"And how about you call me at this number on this card if you remember anything else?"

Walking back across the street to the hotel, Robert spoke as he walked, but Gates didn't catch it.

"Say again?" Gates asked.

"Get a sundae," Robert repeated.

"Yeah," Gates said, touched by the kid's habit of verifying a promise. He guessed the young man had been deeply disappointed more than a time or two. "Hot fudge or something," Gates reassured.

As he watched Robert walk into the hotel, it surprised him to notice that he cared what Robert thought, cared whether Robert trusted him. He shook his head. He wondered if he might be getting too soft for this work, caring how a possible suspect felt about him.

Gates woke up the next morning with doubts about the father hypothesis. Why would the father pick her up at school when she had her car there? He didn't know she had driven? He needed to stop her immediately before she told someone something? Her faculty advisor and her friends said she hadn't seemed at all upset or worried that day.

Gates went to his laptop in the study to see whether the profile on the father that he had requested from Riverton Police had been e-mailed. It was there.

> PARKER, DAVID MARION
> Vice president of the Cascade Valley Bank,
> continuous employment for the past twenty-four
> years. No arrests. Long-standing member in
> Rotary and Leadership Council. Board member
> of two local social service organizations.

So far, Gates thought, none of that eliminated him. During his time as a law officer, Gates had seen that molesters, murderers, thieves came from all social strata. In fact, often the higher the status they achieved, the more clever they were at concealing their crimes.

He read on.

> Married, twenty-one years' duration. Two
> children: Jack, a nineteen-year-old sophomore
> at St. Mary's College, Bay Area; Nikki, a sixteen-
> year-old junior at Canyon High.

Vehicles: 2004 Buick Park Avenue, dark green, license 6 CAH 439; 2003 Toyota Highlander, burgundy, license 5 RDM 393; 1999 Camry, silver with gold trim, license 2 KDJ 244; 1996 Ford 150 pickup, gray-black two-tone, 6F 65970.

The report didn't sound any alarms for Gates. He guessed the Buick was Parker's, the Highlander, his wife's. He knew the Camry was the girl's. The profile and statement didn't seem in any way unusual. He was well acquainted with Drummond and the two other men RPD had assigned to the case. They were thorough.

Gates had worked with Drummond once or twice before. He knew the man was dedicated and rigorously honest. He was one of those men who is always physically tight, as if he were holding in his belly and doing isometrics. Gates could imagine him twisting on the steering wheel with his grip when he drove places.

He called Drummond at the department.

"Hey, it's Gates."

"Rome, how's it?"

"Hey, I'm following up some stuff on the Parker thing."

"New stuff?"

"Maybe, but I don't know if it's any good yet."

"Maybe you'd let me decide that?"

"Sure." Gates felt he had to protect Compton. If police came after him, he would probably close up like an oyster. "Uh, street word around the County; I'm over there a day or so a week at the competency hearings."

"Go."

"Yeah, hearsay, maybe a white car, maybe a mature man arguing with the girl inside the car, maybe hit her and drove off."

"That's pretty goddamn specific, Rome. Who you been talking to?"

"Drum, really, it's just rumor right now, but I'm all over it. I'll call the minute I have something solid. It's your case, dead clear."

"Don't say 'dead.'"

"Right. Hey, you interviewed the dad in November?"

"You like the dad for this!"

"No. No. God, calm down."

"Go."

"Okay, you talked to the dad. Any feeling about him?"

"A ghost. Insane with grief. Looked ninety years old."

"Hey, mind if I talk to him again?"

"Shit on a post, Gates. What you got? Give it up!"

"You'll be the first, Drum, I swear it. I got to go."

As soon as Gates hung up, his phone started ringing. Probably Drummond. He ignored it and hoped that it wasn't a mistake talking to the man. This case was making everybody crazy. Possibly himself, too. He gave up on the father idea, it wasn't panning out, and sent Drummond an e-mail to that effect. No sense making him edgier than he already was.

At 3:30, Bruce was knocking on Robert's door.

"Come on. Let's go to the store."

Robert said "Rite Aid" through the door. He couldn't help himself.

Bruce tried the door. It opened and Robert was standing right there, just as he had been for the past fifteen minutes.

"Hiya!" Bruce was smiling and cheerful as usual.

"Hi." Robert wondered if he was glad to see the new guy. He didn't even think about the movie. Too big a step.

"You like candy?"

Robert nodded.

"All right! Let's roll!" Bruce headed down the stairs, towing Robert loosely by the sleeve of his ski jacket.

The movie itself was way louder than Robert expected. He hadn't been to one since high school and didn't remember them being so noisy.

"Dolby Digital!" Bruce explained. "Just like really being there right in the middle of the action!"

Robert had not been able to keep up with the plot twists and didn't want to ask Bruce and get a lecture in the theater, but he did like the cars. The races and the chases were exciting. And the girls! A really pretty one had showed her chest. Robert decided right then to go back to the Arcade Newsstand after work tomorrow.

Walking back to the hotel, he tuned Bruce out. Bruce had been talking nonstop since the film ended.

Robert knew if he hadn't gone he would have been sleeping

part of the time and walking the rest of the time, and here he was walking anyway. And he had had some good candy. And the movie itself was okay.

Since high school, and Robert could hardly remember back then, he hadn't had a friend, except for his pals on the ward at Chico. Maybe he and Bruce were pals. Robert shrugged to get his shoulders to relax. And soon that other guy was going to take him to get ice cream. Maybe this town wasn't so bad after all.

The crypts were littered with dead insects and dry leaves, empty but for the coffins sealed on shelves within. They smelled like dust and old plaster. Dead ends.

When Janochek went back to the cottage, Pearl and Murray agreed to meet Saturday morning and thoroughly search the whole place—trees, shrubbery, outbuildings, even roofs, from the top corner of the property all the way down to the city street.

They found some strange stuff: a plastic grocery sack containing two rolls of toilet paper beside a mildewed sleeping bag, hidden in a thicket by the fence bordering the rodeo grounds. In the newer section, deep in juniper bushes, a corkscrew, a rusty pocketknife, and some empty cough syrup bottles.

They didn't find a body.

Saturday afternoon, Murray went seeking the new voice. The winter sun was weak, but he figured he still had at least an hour of daylight left. He began on the last two lanes from the road, which he hadn't covered yet.

He walked slowly and quietly, focusing.

Near the end of the haphazard row of markers on the second-to-last lane, he thought he heard something. He stopped and made his breathing quiet. Crying, soft crying. He could barely hear it. Like a big radar dish, Murray turned around very slowly, trying to see if he could get a stronger signal in any direction.

He heard it better when he was about due east, pointed toward the last lane over in this new section. He turned around one more time. Yes, confirmed. Then he did something he didn't like to do, especially in the daylight. He walked straight for the sound, right over the top of other people's graves.

Murray wound up behind a shiny charcoal granite headstone. When he stopped, he could hear a girl's voice. And along with it now, he could hear moaning. He was getting queasy. He had never felt this way before with Dearly or any of the others. The sounds came in waves, and somewhere in there, in the background, the more he tuned in, he could hear yells or screams. Like someone was being hurt. He had a strong urge to back up, to leave.

It reminded Murray of the time he had been awakened by sounds, terrible sounds, coming from his mom's room. Moans and cries and yelling. And he had run in to save her. But she wasn't being hurt exactly. Or maybe she was. But she and the guy she was with got mad and told Murray to get the hell out. Leave them alone! And Murray had spent the rest of that night in a sleeping bag in his backyard.

The longer Murray stood close to the headstone, the louder the noise became. He remembered a time last year when he was walking to school. At a big intersection, a mom with kids in her car had run a red light. She plowed into a big SUV. Murray heard the bang and looked up. The cars were smashed together and a hubcap was rolling down the street. All the traffic stopped and there was silence. Until a couple of the kids started yelling. Wailing. A dazed girl held a badly broken arm out the window, screaming. And another girl was moaning for her mother, who looked dead against the steering wheel. Those cries haunted Murray for months after.

This sound was like that. Like something horrible had happened . . . or was going to happen right now—

Murray ran. Like a coward, he ran.

When Janochek got back from his Saturday-afternoon bike ride, Pearl was sitting in their living room, writing on a pad of lined paper. She told him that she was working on the cemetery project, but her teacher had said it might not have to be a paper after all, maybe just an oral report. She told him she was writing things down anyway, making some notes so she wouldn't forget anything he had said.

As he listened, Janochek found he still didn't quite believe her, but he didn't want to question her further and seem like he was doubting her.

She waited for him to sit in his favorite reading chair, faded maroon and round-armed, with a matching ottoman. "I think this paper or this talk, whatever it turns out to be, would be even more interesting if I had something special or something strange to say about cemeteries."

Janochek noticed that Pearl had managed to morph this "paper" into some vague assignment that would give her an excuse to put him off in case he asked to read her work.

"Did people ever use cemeteries to hide things?" Pearl asked.

He immediately wondered aloud if Jewish people had ever been sheltered in crypts to keep the Nazis from finding them. And artworks. Maybe books? The Gnostic Gospels in the caves. Were they also burial grounds?

"Do we have any caves in this cemetery?"

Why was she suddenly so interested in this place,?

"Pearl, I keep having this feeling there's something you're not telling me."

"God, Dad, you're such a parent sometimes."

"Don't curse! Of course I'm a parent. I'm your damn father."

"Dad."

"All right. All right. But, (a) I'm supposed to be a parent, and (b) you shifted the subject to me. What I want to know is if there's something you're not telling me."

"Jeez, Dad, you'd think I was a criminal or something. Just forget about it!"

She went into her bedroom and shut the door. End of discussion.

Janochek had seen this performance before.

Murray couldn't think of anyplace to go but home. He really did not want to think about what had just happened. It was like the joke: count to ten without thinking of rabbits. Once somebody said that to you, as soon as you started counting, you automatically thought about rabbits. He sang instead. Some Christmas carols he had learned years ago in school. They were comforting, and besides, they were the only songs he knew.

The front door was unlocked. Inside, Murray's mom was sitting at the dining-nook table with a man in dark pants, a white shirt, and a narrow black tie. They both turned to look at him. The man wore glasses and had bad posture. Murray knew a thing or two about posture because his gym teacher had used him as a bad example. Murray thought the man looked like a Gumby.

"Murray, you know Frank, don't you?" his mom asked.

Murray didn't say anything. Then he realized he had stopped walking, and he started again, moving toward his room.

"Murray. Murray! Stop for a minute. I want to ask you something."

Of all the days! But he stopped.

"Frank has just offered to take me and you out to dinner. I haven't seen you in a while, and I want you to come."

Murray reassessed the white shirt and tie. What if this was a government guy? He could not remember his mom ever inviting him to dinner with one of her men. He couldn't think what was going on, but he was reluctant to risk messing it up.

"Where are you going?" he asked.

His mom turned to Frank. Frank looked at her and then back at Murray.

"Where would you like to go?" he asked Murray.

Sheesh! Murray couldn't remember going anywhere except fast-food places. Denny's for breakfast once.

"Uh, Denny's?"

"Sure," Frank said, as if that was a great idea. "Denny's it is! Ready?" he asked, looking from Murray to his mom.

Frank stood and put on the sport coat that had been hanging on the back of his chair.

"Frank is a Pentecostal minister who just moved up here from Fresno," she said, to no one in particular, as they walked out the door. "I met him today in the line at Safeway. He's going to settle down and stay in Riverton, aren't you, Frank?"

Murray didn't hear Frank's response. He had walked fast out to the sidewalk, trying to spot what Frank was driving. Looking for clues. What was his mom doing this time?

Frank took them to the Denny's by the freeway. His mom had talked constantly all the way in the car, and when they picked a booth and sat in it, there was finally a moment of silence. Frank broke it.

"Well . . . ," he said, looking across the table at Murray.

"Murray." Mom supplied the name to him.

"Murray," he said. "I'm not embarrassed to say that I've taken a shine to your mom. She's the friendliest person I've met in the week I've been here." He paused, looking for confirmation or something.

Murray held his look but didn't say anything.

"As your mom told you, I'm a godly man, and I've always believed friendliness is next to godliness!" He chuckled then, and Mom followed suit.

Murray didn't get it.

Frank looked over at her, and then back at Murray.

"What she didn't tell you is that I'm going to be the new youth minister at Valley Pentecostal, over on the east side. The *youth minister*," he emphasized, "so I'm hoping you and I might get along as well as your mom and I seem to."

His smile was too big.

Thank God, the waitress came right then and handed them menus and asked if they wanted anything to drink. Murray buried his face in the laminated pages and didn't surface again until she asked for their order. By that time, Frank and his mom had started talking together. He heard his mom tell the man that he, Murray, was a good boy but real shy and to just give him time and Murray would warm up to him. Frank said that, for right now, a deacon had given him a room in his home, but that he was looking for his own apartment and expected to have one by the first of January.

Frank told her that he loved kids, had always wanted a family, but that he had decided to wait to date anyone until he was out of the service and finished courses at the Pentecostal Bible College in Fresno. He'd finished up in October, got his assignment to Riverton in mid-November, and here he was. And since he had done the things he'd set out to do, he would like Mom to consider being his first formal date, maybe dinner, just the two of them, early next week.

Mom asked him what this was, meaning tonight, and he said it was just a simple courtesy for being so open and polite to him at the "big impersonal supermarket." He told her, "You know, God works in mysterious ways." Murray thought, This guy sure can talk; maybe he really is a preacher.

During the meal, Murray kept his eyes on his plate, staying out of the conversation. He was trying to zone out and not think about the cemetery. He did hear one other thing, though. Frank said he was going to be giving the convocation tomorrow morning and invited them to attend.

Sunday morning started with sunshine bright enough to penetrate the windows and wake him. Murray lay in bed dreading the day, particularly the afternoon, when he would meet Pearl and have to tell her about yesterday. Did he have to tell her? He thought it over. It hadn't worked before to try to keep anything from her. Murray really didn't want to go back to that gravestone. But maybe he'd feel better with Pearl there. He wanted to talk to Dearly first, he knew that.

He got up and went to the bathroom and then to the kitchen. As usual, he glanced at his mom's bedroom door. It wasn't shut! The bed was made and there were no clothes strewn around the floor. He heard her then, in the kitchen. *Jeez*. He tried to think when the last time was he'd seen her act like a homemaker.

"Feel like going to church?" she called as soon as she saw him.

Church! That was a new one. And then he remembered last night.

Okay, now he understood why this dressed-and-breakfast thing might be happening.

His mom asked, "Want an egg?"

She was boiling some, and he could smell toast.

"Yeah, please."

"I want to hear Frank," she said. "He may be the nicest guy I've come across in ages, and I think he likes me, likes us."

After Murray's experience at the tombstone yesterday, he supposed church wouldn't be such a bad idea, but he didn't want to go. He wasn't ready to go back to the cemetery until around noon. He guessed staying home by himself was the default decision.

"Um, thanks, Mom, but no thanks. I've got some homework I need to get done so I'm just going to stay here." Since his mother never asked him about school, she had no way to evaluate his excuse.

Her hair was in curlers during breakfast, but by the time she left, she had brushed it out to a curly sheen. She was wearing a modest blue dress, stockings, and medium heels. Murray thought she looked real nice.

Monday morning at eight, Billup walked up the stairs and into the station, ready for work. He nodded to the duty officer in front and started for the stairs to his cubicle.

"Hold it," the duty officer said. It was Webber today, and he was holding his hand up like *stop*.

"Whaddayamean?" Billup was embarrassed and hoped no one was listening.

"Fowler said to stop you if you came in and to tell you to leave for now and report to his office at one."

"I work here." *You dumb shit.*

"I know you do," Webber said, his face reddening.

"And Fowler told you to tell me this?"

Webber met his stare.

Billup wanted to feel outrage. He wanted to show his incredulity, but while he was driving to the station, he had already envisioned the possibility of something like this happening. Best to pretend like it was just par for the course. Like he was on special assignment. If they fired him, if they really went so far as to fire him over this crap, he would leave this stupid job and work for Sierra West security or, hell, even ARCO Arena security and get in to see all the Kings games free. He didn't need this shit.

He'd come back at one, but if Fowler was a dick, or they wanted him to beg to be reinstated, piss on 'em. He could get a job anywhere.

When he came back in at 12:55, nobody said squat to him. He went upstairs to Fowler's office without stopping at his own. Fowler sat at his desk, eating a sandwich. He motioned for Billup to come in, and put down his sandwich. He dug through the jumble of papers on his desk and selected an oversized manila envelope. He drew out a report, three or four pages typed and stapled, and briefly riffled through the pages. He hadn't asked Billup to sit.

Billup knew he was screwed. He could see by the way he was being treated. Goddamn that Brenda! And the fat therapist bitch! He'd like to see this skinny bastard Fowler with that therapist. She'd tie his bony little neck in a twist, too, ignorant know-it-all bastard.

"Waldrop is the Employee Assistance Profesional for the whole department." Fowler talked as he read. "Her report recommends immediate referral to alcohol treatment."

"That's horseshit, Dave."

"Lieutenant."

"Lieutenant . . . uh, she saw me for a few minutes and she already had her mind made up. She's a man-hater."

Fowler sat holding the report. He did not respond.

"Damn it! All right, all right. I'll start some weekly therapy, once a week. You recommend the person."

Fowler continued to look at the report. "It says nix on psychotherapy. Says minimum a month clean and sober, first. Clearly recommends an alcohol/drug program; suggests thirty days at Mulcahey's in Calistoga.

"I already checked. Our insurance covers it. So I am continuing your suspension, keeping your medical benefits active, and very strongly encouraging you to enroll at Mulcahey's. The suspension will remain in effect until I receive written confirmation that you have successfully completed the thirty-day, continuous alcohol treatment. Any questions?"

"For shit's sake, Dave—Lieutenant—this isn't even legal."

"Vern, I am not going to argue. I've established a paper trail on you that is substantial. You may be prosecuted, should Brenda choose to, along with the department, for sexual harassment. If you decline to comply with this directive, termination is my next option."

Billup was too angry to speak. He was fighting the urge to climb over Fowler's desk and beat him to a pulp. He stormed out of the office, down the stairs, and out of the building. He needed some breathing room!

Billup drove to Cottonwood, to the bar by the stockyards where he didn't think he'd see anybody he knew. He was livid! What was it with people? Why were they out to screw him? It took three refills with draft chasers before he could calm down enough to think.

He hated Fowler, always had. Take Brenda's word over his like a chickenshit. But it was the EAP bitch who had buried him. And Brenda. *God! Women!* Why couldn't they just let him do his work? Help the homeless, get hookers off the streets, get that geeky little bastard out of the cemetery and into juvenile hall, where he belonged.

He decided to have another bump, maybe some single malt, and then bring the wrath of justice down! He realized he kind of liked his rage. It pumped him up. *A treatment program, my ass!*

Murray was sitting with Edwin, waiting for Pearl, when she came down from the workshop. She plopped down next to him. "What's new? Anything yesterday afternoon?"

Murray had thought about how he wanted to tell her, thought about leaving out the part about how scared he was. But he decided that she needed to know, needed to understand . . . what? That he might flip out again? Well, at least she needed to know that if he ran again, it wasn't anything she did. And she should know just to let him run.

He told her. He could see that what he said scared her a little, too.

"Man," she said, "what do you think it is?"

"I'm not sure," he said. "I'm hearing a girl crying like she's in pain, and moaning, some kind of moaning. I mean, I've heard voices before, but not like that. It's spooky. I don't know how . . . I'm . . . I don't even know that I can help." He was reaching for words. "I can't explain it."

They didn't say anything for a bit.

"So, do you want to come with me?" He amended, "I mean, *will* you come with me?"

"Should I tell my dad where we're going to be, in case anything happens?"

"No. No, this is too weird. Nothing major's going to happen." He rubbed the back of his neck. "Except I may get scared again. If I do, you go home, we meet tomorrow. Okay?"

When she didn't reply, Murray started walking slowly across the graves. He could feel Pearl walking behind him.

Maybe I can't hear any voice when she's with me. About three feet from the dark gray tombstone, the hair on his arms began to stand up.

He could hear it.

Groaning, crying. "Help me! Please find me! Please find me! Please."

Where was the moaning coming from? Were the screams an echo? It seemed like several sounds running together. What if he disappeared in these sounds? Couldn't bring his mind back? He felt like he was fizzing, bubbling inside.

Pearl took hold of his arm. The sounds gradually receded. The sound he was hearing was himself, he realized . . . at least there at the end.

Pearl moved up to stand close beside him. He could feel her heartbeat.

"Are you okay?" she asked. "Are you okay? Do you want to go?"

No. Murray wanted to walk around to the front of the tombstone. He wanted to see what was on it. But he wanted her to keep holding his arm.

"Would you stay close like this and walk around to the other side with me?" he asked her.

"Sure," she said.

They went around. Murray read the name.

WILLIAM TAYLOR CRADDOCK
PRECIOUS HUSBAND — LOVING FATHER

That can't be right!
"What?" Pearl said.

He realized he had said it aloud. "I said, I don't see how that could be right. I was hearing a girl's voice." He wanted to argue with the inscription. *It doesn't fit. It isn't right.* But he didn't want to go close to the stone again. "Let's walk," he said. "Let's take a break for a while."

Farther up the hill, past the angel, they started talking.

"What do you do at school?" he asked Pearl.

"Oh, not much," she said. "I take accelerated English and freshman Spanish. I have some friends but I'm not popular. I'm on the basketball team but I'm not great, so I don't score much in the games, but I hang in there on defense and I get some rebounds."

"How about you?" she asked. "What are you like at school?"

"Ah, jeez, you don't want to know. I do okay in classes but not real well. I don't care too much about school. Some of the assholes hassle me, but mostly people just ignore me, leave me alone."

"Did you tell them to do that? You told me to do that."

"No. I don't know. Some kids teased me about my mother."

"Why?"

"She's been arrested before. She goes out with a lot of guys. Kids call her names and we argue and then they call me names."

"My mom went out with other guys, too. A lot, I think," Pearl said, "even though she was married."

Murray was surprised. He hadn't imagined Janochek would have a wife like that. He reached out and almost touched her shoulder.

"So," Pearl said, "want to talk about it?"

"No," he said.

"What do you think's going on?"

Murray shook his head.

"Did you hear the voice?"

"Yeah, but there was other noise with it. I could hear this girl's voice saying 'help me, please find me.'"

"You're going to help her, aren't you?" Pearl asked.

Murray thought of the words he had wanted on his tombstone: *Friend to the Deceased.*

"I don't know how," he said. "It doesn't make any sense."

"Do you think Craddock did something to her?"

"The dead guy? No. I don't think so. I mean, she didn't say so. I mean, I really just don't know."

Murray looked around. Not that many people came up here to visit. This was the oldest section, and Murray thought most of the loved ones who would mourn here were themselves long gone. The old graves were crumbly and peaceful. The trees above them were bare, their branches like spider webs.

"Do you want me to talk to my father about this?"

"I don't think so," he said, coming back to earth. "What would you say?"

"I could ask him about Craddock."

"Yeah, okay, you could try that, I guess, but don't tell him anything else. Okay?"

"Sure. I mean, okay. I won't. Want to go to the work-shop for a while? The woodstove is probably going, and we could get a glass of water or something. I wouldn't ask my dad anything while you're there, if he's around."

"Will he mind if I'm there?"

"No. I think he likes you. The poor misguided man!"

That evening after dinner, Pearl asked her dad. They were both reading, Pearl lying on the couch and her dad in a recliner in the corner of their small living room.

"Dad, do you know anything about that guy Craddock who's buried down in the newer part?"

"No," he said, resting his book on the arm of the chair. "Survived by a wife and two children, if I remember right. I don't know what killed him, if that's what you mean. Why do you ask?"

"Oh, uh, Murray thinks he knows . . . or might know a girl who's buried around here somewhere and we were just walking and looking in the newer section today, and I saw Craddock's marker."

"That pretty gray one, nearly black with silver flecks. I think they bought that special. Ordered it from a place in Oregon. Granite with mica in it."

"Dad, uh, do they ever make mistakes?"

"What do you mean?"

"Put the wrong name on a stone or put somebody in the wrong place?"

"Oh, I'm sure they do sometimes. Spell the name wrong. We've had that happen here." He laughed. "Once, unfortunately, to a woman whose last name was Cutter. The stonemason made it 'Gutter.' Not a happy family!"

"How about put somebody in the wrong place?"

"I suppose it's theoretically possible, if there were two or three burials on the same day, and the people present had not bought the plot themselves, so they didn't know where the grave was supposed to be located. Or maybe days after the burial, the stonemason could unknowingly put the marker over the wrong person. Or, I guess a funeral home might mix up two nearly identical closed coffins, but it would be rare. Really rare."

"How many people were buried the day Craddock was?"

"Pearl, what is this thing about Craddock?"

"Nothing, Dad. Just curious. How many?"

"Pearl, for crying out loud, I don't remember stuff like that. We have over a thousand people here."

"Isn't it easy to find out? To look up?"

"Saints in heaven, Pearl. If I look it up, will you leave me in peace and let me read my damn book?"

"Sure, Dad. I'm sorry. I didn't mean to bug you. I'm just curious."

Janochek set his book on the end table and went out the side door to his file cabinet in the workshop. He was back in a minute or so. "William Craddock was the only person buried that day, October seventeenth. Him and nobody else here at this cemetery. Satisfied?"

"How about from the mortuary to the church service? Could they have mixed up the body then?"

"Pearl!"

"Well, could they?"

"Great Caesar's ghost!"

Janochek got up again and stomped to his computer. He got on the Web to access the newspaper, searched obituaries during mid-October, and scanned them until he found Craddock's.

142

"Died at home, natural causes, believed heart attack. Died overnight in bed. No reason to have a closed-casket funeral unless he had gone to the trouble to put it in his will, or maybe the wife couldn't face him in death. But his service was attended by his family. Almost certainly open casket at the viewing, possibly even at the service.

"Let's see. Service was at the mortuary down the street. They're the people who prepared him. From the mortuary, carried by pallbearers to the hearse and then to here. I would say no possibility of a mix-up."

"Thanks, Dad."

He did not reply. She knew he wouldn't. She could always read him like a book.

Pearl, bouncing with energy, found Murray with James.

"I talked to my dad last night about the Craddock stone," she said. "It's him, all right. No one else was buried that day, so there couldn't have been a mix-up. The same people took him straight from the funeral home to the cemetery."

"You checked all that out?"

"Yeah. Or, I mean, Dad did. He said mix-ups were very rare and only likely to happen when multiple burials are going on. The voice you're hearing is probably coming from another plot, close by. Start where you left the path yesterday and go on around the corner and then all the way back to the main road and I'll be right beside you."

"When I'm listening, don't touch me."

"Sure, okay."

Murray felt edgy as soon as they got to the part of the lane behind the dark tombstone. He thought he could hear those sounds again, but he didn't try to tune into them yet. The sounds got fainter as he rounded the corner, stronger as he moved up the last lane that passed in front of Craddock. He shuddered. The wailing became gradually softer as he walked slowly back to the main road. At the intersection, Murray stopped and tuned up his listening. He could still hear it, very dim, no clear words.

He headed back to Craddock's marker and turned to Pearl.

"It's here," he said. "I'm pretty sure."

"It can't be," Pearl said.

"I think it is."

"Sit down in front of it and touch it," she said.

God! I'd rather be shot. He made himself sit.

Murray pictured being electrocuted as soon as he touched that stone. He took a deep breath and waited for Pearl to sit down beside him. Then he reached out and touched the stone in front, next to the name.

Murray did feel a charge, but it wasn't like an electric shock, exactly. More like a dial tone, or when they turned the PA system on in the gym and you could hear a faint hiss and buzz. Right away he heard her.

"Found me. You found me." The moaning faded. Her voice was weak, like she was exhausted.

"I heard you, and I've been looking for you," Murray said.

Crying again.

"He killed me."

Murray didn't know what to say.

"He hit me. I couldn't breathe."

Murray could hardly stand to listen.

"He killed me!" Sobs. Hiccuping. "He killed me! And he wanted to cut me up in smaller pieces so he could get rid of me."

Murray let go of the stone and fell back.

"Breathe!" Pearl was yelling at him. "Come on! Take a breath!"

And he did, and then he was breathing hard, as if he had been running again.

"What happened?" she asked. She was holding him. Supporting him.

Murray told her.

Pearl was quiet until he caught his breath. "Can you find out what happened next?" she asked.

Murray got to his feet and Pearl did the same. He wanted her to understand what it was like for him . . . but she couldn't. Nobody could. Except maybe Dearly and Blessed and Edwin. Murray had never felt so alone. He pictured a paper sack filled with sadness and fear, blowing down streets and through empty places. It didn't belong to anybody, didn't have any substance. Somebody's trash.

"You going to run?" Pearl asked him.

Murray erupted. "These people need me. Everybody needs a friend!" That's what Murray thought. But his heart was churning with fear.

Pearl took a step back, uncertain. Waiting.

Murray sat again and Pearl followed his lead. Murray closed his eyes and put his hands out slowly, until both were touching the stone. This time there was no buzzing. Maybe the softest sound of ocean. He waited. She began to speak.

She told him the guy offered her a ride. She knew him and it was raining and he asked if she was going to her car. When she said yes, he said he would drive her to it. She was in good spirits, thinking about the game the next day, and she got in. He asked her if he could talk to her, and she felt sorry for him. While she was answering, he put his arm around her, touching her shoulder and neck. That was so out of line that she shoved his arm away without even thinking. He got mad and said he needed her to listen to him for a minute, but he kept getting close to her. He put his arm out like he was reaching for her breast and she shoved his hand away as hard as she could. He reacted with a kind of

146

karate move and fired the side of his hand at her, but her arm was lower and he hit her in the throat instead. And after that, she couldn't breathe. It was horrible. It was probably like drowning. And she suffocated and died and nobody knew it. Nobody even knew where she was.

When he got her here, beside the grave, he pulled at her clothes, but it was raining and muddy and he stopped. Then he took out his pocketknife and sawed at her hip like maybe he could take her legs off and make her body smaller and more manageable, but it wouldn't work, so he gave up.

She said the guy laid his head down on her in the rain and started moaning. And then she faded away and everything went black for a long time. And then she started calling for help. It seemed like forever until Murray found her.

"I didn't think anyone ever would," she told him.

Murray tried to picture her, like he did the others, but he couldn't. Maybe he was too tired. Or maybe she was too tired. He took his hands off the stone.

Pearl stayed beside him. She didn't say anything. Murray felt so sleepy. After a while, he turned around and told her what the girl had said. When he finished, they were quiet again. They had lost their energy.

"Everybody knew about it, everybody talked about it." Murray was thinking out loud.

"It's Nikki Parker, isn't it?" she said.

That's when he started crying.

Pearl held Murray while he wept. Not tight or anything. Just held him, and didn't squirm or try to talk him out of it. She didn't say a word. After he settled down, she said, "I've got to ask my dad one more thing."

"What?"

"Can you put two bodies in one coffin?" she asked. And just like that she got it.

Gates was waiting in the car with the window down when Robert walked out of TacoBurger. Robert seemed to be in a reverie; he would have walked right past without even seeing Gates, if Gates hadn't said his name. But when Robert looked, there was no recognition. He was wide-eyed, staring at the car, and then he started running out the back lot. Gates lost sight of him when he cut around a building.

Gates was still sitting there, wondering what had happened. He didn't think Robert had even looked at him.

The car. Gates was in a white sheriff's unmarked Crown Vic with a whip antenna, one of the two departmental general staff cars. The big white car Robert had mentioned. *He looked like you.*

Gates started the car and drove back to the office to check the transportation logs. He would give Robert time to recover before he contacted him again.

At the office, he looked at the records for October 17, the day the Parker girl disappeared. The other Ford, last year's model, was not checked out that day. The car he had been driving today, a '99 four-door Ford Crown Victoria scheduled for replacement before too long, was checked out for that whole day to Betty O'Meara in admin, to go to an accounting services workshop in Lakeport, two to three hours southwest. Car checked out at six o'clock in the morning. Checked back in at 6:45 p.m. by dispatcher clerk Mona Andrews.

Gates called Mona at home. He apologized for bothering her on her day off, but asked her if, by any chance, she remembered checking in the Crown Vic from Betty O. on an evening in mid-October. She said she'd have to see the log to get the right date for sure, but yes, she remembered the incident because she had joked with Betty about trying to pile up comp time driving around the state, and Betty had said something like, "You'll never guess how much fun a woman can have at a rural accounting workshop," and they had both laughed. Mona asked what this was about and Gates assured her it had nothing to do with Betty. It was just a vehicle survey at this point, and he would have more for her later.

Gates called Drummond.

"Go."

"I have some reason to believe that the vehicle that picked up the Parker girl at the school is a white government-type car. Unmarked, or maybe one with a small sign like the county seal on the side. Maybe with a whip antenna, if there are any of those still in service."

"What reason to believe?"

"I have been developing a source in the mental health community, a fragile source, trust me on this, who may have witnessed the abduction. He bolted today when he saw a car like the one I described."

"Pretty thin."

"I know it's thin. I said I'd call if I got anything at all. You feel like checking for any such vehicles your people checked out on 10/17?"

"Don't tell me my goddamn job."

"Drum, a little touchy lately? Your shrink on vacation?"

"Yeah, yeah. Hey, sorry. I'm really wound tight on this

150

Parker thing. I'm getting heat every day—the mayor, my lieutenant, the press, the whole circus. You know."

"Yeah, I think I do. Give me a call if you turn anything, and I'm going to check Social Services, DA's office, marshal's office, local hazardous transport companies, downtown County Admin, county motor pool. Any agency that might be driving something like that."

"Okay. Great. Find me if anything pops."

Gates was already rooting around in his desk drawers for a County directory.

Murray was asleep in the big chair close to the woodstove in the workshop. Pearl was thinking about something her dad had told her when he was talking about the history of cemeteries. They stacked them up, he had said. One on top of the other.

So, Pearl thought, the Craddocks buried their Precious Husband and Loving Father during the day of the seventeenth and somebody put the Parker girl's body in there with him that night. The ground would be loose. Humped up over the grave. A person could lay a blanket or a tarp down next to the plot and put the dirt on it as he shoveled. And then practically pour it back in when he was done. Dig down to the coffin. Dump the body in the hole. Cover it back up and, voilà, done deal. Gosh, she thought, it fit what Dearly had said. Hide it in plain sight. It wasn't exactly in plain sight, but it was in a fresh grave where a fresh grave was supposed to be. Brilliant! And nobody would have ever been the wiser if it hadn't been for our old grave-talker over there.

But the next step had Pearl stumped. What to do now? Was this the point where she would finally let her dad in on the deal? She decided to wake Murray and ask him.

"He'll want to know why we think so" was Murray's first concern.

"I've thought of that. We'll say that, a month ago, when you were hanging out here, you saw somebody messing around with that gravesite, digging or something, when the dirt was still fresh. You didn't think too much about it at the time, but since then, you've seen him messing around a couple more times and you think maybe he put something he shouldn't have in Craddock's grave."

"Him?"

"Yeah, say a man. That will make it more believable."

"Well, I don't want to be here when you tell him. I don't want him questioning me. You tell him tonight. And see if you can get him to do something, and I'll see you at the angels after school tomorrow."

"Deal."

While they were eating one of Pearl's favorites, canned chili with extra hamburger and sweet cherry peppers, Pearl told her father that she needed to talk to him. He put his spoon aside and gave her his complete attention. She starting by apologizing for possibly acting a little strange sometimes lately. She said she had been working on kind of a mystery with Murray and that something really upsetting had come up that she knew her dad would want to know about. She said that Murray had seen someone messing around at Craddock's grave, more than once. The first time was right around when the Parker girl disappeared, and Pearl was afraid that the girl might be buried with Craddock, hidden, and she didn't know what to do.

"Lord of the furry and feathered!" Janochek paused, pushed back in his chair, eyebrows raised, skeptical. But that expression faded, quickly followed by a softer look of concern.

"So the crypt thing was just looking to see if someone had stuck her in there?"

Pearl appeared to think that over and come to some kind of decision.

"In a way, yeah, I guess maybe we thought someone had stashed a body in one of those places. But then we didn't know it was the Parker girl."

"*We* thought! Did Kiefer put you up to this?"

"No, Dad! I *made* him tell me about it. It's not his fault at all. Please don't blame him or be mad at him for anything. He's really nice, and he did everything he could to keep me from being involved. That's what we were fighting about at first. I mean, that's why I was so mad at him. He wouldn't tell me anything. Not a thing. I practically forced him to."

Janochek could imagine that. Kiefer had never seemed manipulative. But Pearl . . . .

"All right, why do you think this is about the Parker girl?"

Pearl looked stricken. She didn't say anything for a moment. She seemed to be stalling. She's concocting another damn story, Janochek thought.

"Well . . . well, uh, what does everybody know about the Parker girl's disappearance?"

Janochek was watching Pearl very closely. He thought he could see small beads of perspiration on her forehead.

"Uh, the high school," she said, thinking out loud. "She probably was taken from the high school, um, probably by a man, wouldn't you think? And she was probably taken . . . Didn't she go missing a few weeks ago, around the middle of October? And Craddock—"

Janochek got up and went to his computer.

"October seventeenth," he said. "That's the day she went missing. Same day Craddock was buried." He looked over at Pearl still sitting at the dining table. "That's one bloody hell of a coincidence," he said, closing his eyes and taking some very deep breaths.

After a while, he came back to the table.

"Let me think about this tonight and we'll talk about it again tomorrow morning." Before she could respond, he added, "Tomorrow's your last day before the break, isn't it?"

She nodded.

"Okay," he said. "It's waited this long. I'll be here at the shop tomorrow afternoon when you get home from practice and we'll talk about the next step on this. I need to think it over tonight."

But that night he wasn't thinking about the next step. He was thinking how awful it would be if anyone ever took Pearl.

Murray got home a little after dark. It had been drizzling and he was wet and cold. Frank's car was in the driveway behind theirs and the front door was unlocked. Murray hesitated. He didn't like to walk in on his mom. He listened at the door. The TV was on and they were talking. Should be safe.

His mom and Frank were sitting at the dining room table. The house smelled like spaghetti sauce, and they were dishing lettuce out of a salad bowl and putting it on two real plates that Murray had never seen before.

"Murray, honey, dry off and come eat with us. We're having spaghetti. It's one of Frank's favorites. His mother was Italian, and he's been showing me how to cook the . . . what did you call it?" she asked, looking at Frank.

"Pasta," he said through a mouthful of salad.

"Pasta," she echoed. "I'll set a place."

Murray wasn't sure he was hungry after this afternoon, but it did smell good. Something was missing. Paper plates . . . and wine.

"How come no paper plates?"

"Murr," she said, gently chiding. "You don't eat spaghetti on paper plates. You know that. They get all torn up."

News to him. They had never in his memory used anything but paper plates.

"Where's the wine?"

"Murray, sweetie, what do you care? You don't drink it anyway."

"Just curious."

"Frank doesn't drink alcohol. He's a minister, remember, and he tries to set an example for the kids he works with."

Well, that was a first. He hadn't really seen his mom in the last couple of days, but come to think of it, he hadn't seen any bottles around either. And she'd been dressed every time he'd seen her. He went into his room and found himself wishing that this Frank guy would stick around. Frank was good for his mother. So far.

The food was pretty tasty, and he was going to do everything he could to keep the cemetery out of his mind for tonight.

Billup awoke in his bed at first light and immediately started retracing. What had he done last night? He recalled meeting with Fowler and the suspension and the demand that he get thirty days alcohol/drug treatment. And then what? He went to the stockyards bar in Cottonwood. After that? He hoped he just drove home and went to sleep. Damn it!

He was sweating. This was not how he had planned his life. He was going to get married, have a family, have a successful career. So how did he get so sidetracked with all this drinking? He had partied hearty in high school but never got into any particular trouble. This blackout stuff didn't start till after his divorce. No, that's not true. It had happened from time to time even in high school, but never regularly like now.

He was afraid to go to the damn drug program. Afraid he might not be able to stop drinking even if he tried. Somehow he had gotten split off from himself. If what Brenda had said about him was true, that was ugly. He was starting to be like the kind of person he became a police officer to arrest, to get off the streets so the decent people could be safe.

And these nightmares . . . He knew he had thrashed around during the night in some violent, bloody quagmire.

He had lost his marriage and was about to lose his job. He was probably going to tank a recovery program—if he even went. Most of the people he worked with disliked him, avoided him whenever possible. Nobody ever called him at home. He didn't even have bar friends.

God, he wanted a drink. He couldn't stand feeling so

awful, so disgusting. *Here we go again! No! Just say* no! He wasn't going to start that up again. He turned over and put the pillow over his head to block out the daylight.

He wondered whether he actually had the courage to shoot himself.

Robert had run back to his hotel yesterday, looking over his shoulder every few seconds to make sure he wasn't followed.

A big white car with a long radio thing. How did that guy in the car find him at work? Did the guy know he had been talking to the police about him and the girl?

The guy was going to hurt him. Maybe kill him! That's why Robert was going to stay in his room for the next few days. Not even answer if someone knocked. If he lay low, the guy might forget about him.

Robert got very little sleep. The next morning, he realized he couldn't go to work again for a while. He'd have to tell them that he was sick, had the flu. He'd have to go downstairs and ask the manager to call them right now. Before the hitting guy found his hotel. He quietly opened his door and looked up and down the hall. Empty. He left his room and walked to the stairs. Nobody there. He hustled down the steps until he got to the lobby, where he stopped and looked. Same old couple on the couch. What's-his-name at the card tables. Manager must be in his office. Robert lit out for the front desk.

"Robert!"

Robert jumped like he had been shot, and wheeled to face his attacker.

Bruce. Bruce was walking toward him. "Robert. Hey, what's the hurry? How you doin'?"

Robert turned and continued to the front desk and looked in the office for the manager.

"Can you help me?"

The manager looked up from his crossword.

"Um, I'm sick and I can't go to work tomorrow. Will you call my job and tell them?"

"Sure, but how do you know you're going to be sick tomorrow?" But he was talking to Robert's back as Robert hurried back to the stairs, right past Bruce.

"Hey! Hey! Slow down! Robert!" Bruce was left standing in the middle of the lobby as Robert motored back up the stairs.

Gates's search for white four-door motor-pool cars had been fruitless. The County agencies and Social Services had all gone to smaller cars with better gas mileage. Same with the DA's office. The marshal still drove a white four-door Ford with a whip, but it also bore very distinctive green-and-gold striped markings, which would be the first thing anyone would notice. The three hazardous transport companies in this area no longer bought or drove sedans. They had converted over a year ago to four-wheel-drive pickups and SUVs. A dead end.

He hoped Drummond had had better luck. He was going to call him after lunch, but first he was going to see Robert. Robert didn't work today and he ought to be at his hotel. Gates left the office and drove to the Sadler.

On his way across the lobby, somebody spoke to him. Gates stopped. It was the kid Robert had talked to outside the donut place.

"What did you say?" Gates asked.

The kid stood up. "Bruce," he said.

"Bruce," Gates confirmed, nodding.

"I said watch out for Robert. He's wiggy."

"What do you mean?" Gates had been afraid of something like this.

"My man Rob came racing through the lobby about an hour ago and told the manager to tell his job he'd be sick tomorrow. Tomorrow! Then he hustled back upstairs to his room. At least I think he went to his room. He wouldn't answer the door or say anything when I went after him to see if he was okay. You gonna see him now?"

Gates said he had hoped to.

"I don't think he'll talk to you or let you in," Bruce said.

Gates walked over to the hotel office. He pulled out his badge and showed it to the manager as he asked for a passkey.

"I don't expect any trouble at all," he told the man. "But it's very important I speak to Mr. Compton right now."

The manager gave him a key off his chain and Gates went upstairs. He heard Bruce behind him. He blocked Bruce's path on the stairs. "I need to talk with Robert alone first for a few minutes."

"Right. Okay," Bruce said, eager to be helpful. "Tell Robert I said hi. Okay?"

"You bet."

Gates knocked on Robert's door. No response. He talked to Robert through the door and said who he was and that he had enjoyed their steak dinner together and that he wanted to take Robert out for ice cream soon, but that right now, he really needed to see Robert and talk to him for just a couple of minutes. Still no response, but he had the sense that Robert might be listening at the door. Gates told him that he really was a sheriff's deputy, Robert knew that, and he was here to protect Robert. Bruce had said Robert looked a little upset, and Gates was here to make sure Robert was safe.

"Don't come in!"

"Robert, I have the passkey to the room and I have to come in to make sure you're okay. But I won't touch you or harm you in any way."

Gates put the key in the door and opened it quickly. He could hear footsteps hurrying away. When the door was open, he could see Robert across the small room, tugging on his window, trying to open it.

"Robert!" he said loud enough to get his attention. "You are safe now! I won't let anyone hurt you. Easy. Easy. Please turn around and see who I am."

Robert turned to face Gates. He was breathing so fast his shoulders were heaving. Gates had his own hands up, empty, and he stayed where he was in the doorway.

"I won't take one step closer," he told Robert, "until you feel a little better."

They stood together in the room for two or three more minutes without talking. Then Gates saw Robert's eyes move up to a spot behind him. He turned. Bruce.

"Bruce," Gates said, thinking actually this might further break the tension. "Say a quick hello to your friend and then give us a few more minutes, all right? Maybe in a while, the three of us will go over to Lancaster's for some ice cream."

"Great!" Bruce was always on board for ice cream. "Hey, Rob," he said, "glad you're okay. See you in a bit." And he headed back downstairs.

Robert still hadn't spoken.

"Please tell me about what happened yesterday. When you feel like it," Gates said. "You may have seen the car you told me about."

"He's going to kill me, too," Robert said.

"Too?"

"He hit her real, real hard. You don't know."

"I'm going to stop him, Robert. I'm going to keep him from hurting you or anybody else. Tell me about the car."

"He came after me at work. I saw his car and ran."

"Tell me what you saw."

"A big white car with a long silver thing on the top."

"A four-door." Gates stopped. *Don't feed him information.* "What make of car? Do you know?"

"Huh-uh. This country, though. Not one of those foreign ones."

"Do you drive, Robert?"

"Huh-uh. Not since high school."

"Have you ever had a car?"

"No."

"What long thing on the top?"

"A, uh, like a steel wire. Like an aerial thing."

Gates continued to question until it was clear Robert was describing a whip antenna.

"Can you tell me anything else?" he asked.

"He wants to hurt me," Robert said.

"If I tell the manager and the police and the sheriff to protect you for the next couple of days, will you be okay in your room?"

"Yeah, maybe."

"Will you let Bruce visit and play cards or something?"

"Cards are stupid."

"Well, will you at least let him visit?"

Robert agreed, and Gates promised to arrange twenty-four-hour protection from the hotel staff and the police. He also said he would arrange for food to be sent up and asked if burgers and donuts would be okay. By the time Gates left, he felt that the investigation ought to have a new suspect within a couple of days. The type of car Robert was afraid of was pretty unusual in this community. And who was most likely to be driving such a car?

A Riverton law officer.

Back in his car, he immediately called Drummond.

"Did you get my message?" Drummond asked after Gates identified himself.

"No, I've been out of the office," Gates said.

"I think we got the car," Drummond said, "or at least a car on the streets with the right time frame."

"Tell me!" Gates could feel the adrenaline.

"Hold on. You can't do anything yet."

"Right. Okay."

Drummond told him they, RPD, had a motor-pool Ford out on that day, the main ride of a Public Affairs officer named Billup. Records show that Billup kept the car overnight October 17, and didn't return it to the pool until 5:15 PM the eighteenth. Some guys kept a motor-pool car overnight from time to time if they had taken a trip and gotten back late. No big deal. But Billup sort of made a habit of it. "Records show eight overs in the past three months."

"You brought him in yet?"

"Hold it. There's more," Drummond said. "The guy's just been suspended for harassing a female employee at a local bar, A/D treatment mandated."

"Definitely could be our guy." Gates was excited.

"My partner and Webber are searching and bagging the car right now."

"Hold it! Shouldn't it go to the lab at the college?"

"This will be relatively noninvasive. A prelim. Check for prints and hair. We won't actually get in and tear it apart. I got Haggarty pressing for a search warrant on the guy's house, and we'll probably get that by late this afternoon. Billup has no way to guess we're on to him. No close friends in the department that might tip him. No reason to get nervous and run."

"So, you already got a watch on his house, huh?"

"Yeah. Since about 10:30 this morning. He doesn't answer the phone. Could be hung over, maybe even passed out, the way his supe says he chugs. Car's in the driveway."

"What's the make?"

"Light metallic tan Chrysler LHS, 1997, California plate 4 CDI 189."

"Great work, Drum! Keep me posted."

Drummond agreed and Gates hung up and headed back to the office to think things over. On the way, he called dispatch to see if anything needed doing before he got in. Mona told him to hold while she checked. When she came back on, she said it was quiet except that a guy named something-or-other had called for him three times already, requesting a call back. Gates asked her to spell the name.

"Juliet, Alpha, November, Oscar, Charlie, Hotel, Echo, Kilo."

"You're kidding." Gates tried to imagine how to pronounce it.

"No," Mona said, "Henderson upstairs gave me this. He said something like Jan-oh-check."

Gates got the number and called.

After Janochek answered and found it was Gates, he introduced himself as the Forest Grove caretaker and reminded Gates that they had met a couple of years ago at an exhumation.

Gates remembered.

When Janochek told him why he had called, Gates changed course immediately and headed for the cemetery. Good God, he thought, this thing is going to crack.

Janochek ushered Gates into the workshop office and told him about Kiefer and Pearl's investigation. Gates looked astonished. Janochek finished with the coincidence of the burial date and the disappearance date.

"And Kiefer . . ." Gates was sorting the information.

"You know him?"

"I met him and his mom a while ago. . . . And so Kiefer saw somebody messing around the grave a couple of times and then your daughter joined him in finding out whether there might be some monkey business going on here. You weren't aware of any of this?"

"I knew they were up to something, but I had no idea what."

"And how did they pick this grave to begin with?"

"Kiefer told my daughter, Pearl, that he saw somebody, and I quote, 'messing around' the grave and they took it from there. When I thought this whole thing was part of a school assignment—"

"Why did you think that?"

"That's what Pearl told me. At first. Anyway, we looked in all the crypts on the property. They were okay. No sign of funny business, I mean."

Gates looked away, shaking his head.

"What?" Janochek asked.

"Any chance this could be a hoax the kids are pulling?"

Whoa! Janochek thought about his daughter's willfulness and her sometimes stunning deviousness. She might be capable of this kind of stunt. He thought about Kiefer. Poor kid. He could be led. Hard to imagine he would do something to risk getting barred from this cemetery, but then, what might Pearl have offered as an inducement? How much of her mother's blood ran in her veins? He noticed he was feeling nauseated.

He remembered Gates. "Uh, sorry, what was your question?"

"I think you just answered it," Gates said. "I need to talk to those kids immediately—if not yesterday."

"They'll probably be meeting over here this afternoon. Later, after Pearl's basketball practice, somewhere between three-thirty and five."

"Will you be here, too?" Gates asked.

"Yeah. I said I would talk to them more about the idea this afternoon."

"Where is Craddock's grave?" Gates asked.

"Fourth lane on the right, past the front gate, most of the way to the end on the right-hand side," Janochek responded. He had gone to see the plot earlier in the day.

Gates jotted the information in his small notepad. "Let's meet at the gravesite about four-thirty. Don't talk to them about any of this again until I get there. And don't let them know I'm coming." He rammed the notepad back in his pocket. "I'm going to get to the bottom of this. Today!"

Gates noticed his cell phone on the seat next to him as he drove out of the grounds. It was blinking. He called dispatch. Mona told him that Drummond had left an urgent message to get in touch about ten minutes ago, and she phoned Gates when she couldn't reach him on his radio.

Gates called, got through, and identified himself when Drummond came on.

"We might have a small problem."

"No way," Gates said. "That's more than enough cause for a search warrant. Have Haggarty take it to another judge."

"That's not it," Drummond said, sounding irritable, harried.

"So, what's *it*?" Gates asked. He was a little distracted. He had paperwork and a couple of phone calls to make about another case before his cemetery appointment.

"He has two cars."

"What?" Gates said, not understanding.

"He bought a pickup a few weeks ago, but it wasn't up on the DMV sheet yet."

Drummond had his attention now. "Billup?"

"Billup. Are you with me?"

"Brother, am I!"

"They don't see it."

"The stakeout doesn't see any truck, in the driveway, in the garage, along the block?"

"You got it." Drummond seemed to be carrying on another conversation away from the phone at his desk.

Gates pulled over and parked.

"Description?" Gates asked when Drummond was quiet again.

"Light blue, '87 Mazda B2000 Short Bed, 3Y 40494. Camper shell sitting beside his driveway near the back of the house. Should have tipped us off."

"License again?"

"Three, Yankee, four-zero-four-niner-four."

"Got it. BOLO?"

"Yeah, lookout alerts posted to tri-counties police and sheriff, plus highway patrol. Airplanes, the works."

"Relatives, girlfriend?"

"None known in this area. His application says no sibs, parents deceased. Scuttlebutt: bar drinker, no close friends known."

"Knock on his door?"

"Don't want to risk it yet. Should have the warrant within the hour."

"Send him an undercover with a pizza. Or a package."

"You sheriffs watch too much TV! Hey, I gotta go. We're rolling extra cars. Wear your phone and I'll call when anything breaks."

Gates sat at the curb thinking, God! Nothing for eight weeks and today? An avalanche!

Billup really had no choice. He needed to try the A/D program and see if he could reclaim his life. His no-drinking resolve lasted till midmorning. His head was throbbing, his hands were shaking, and his butt was sore from a scouring diarrhea. Okay, he figured, I need some medicine, now.

All morning he had been reviewing his life. It was disgusting and disgraceful. He was glad his folks hadn't lived to see it. His dad had worked a construction job his whole life, until a heart attack felled him in his early sixties. He had been an okay guy and wasn't abusive except on weekends and holidays when he drank all day. At night, every night, he fell asleep in his chair in front of the TV. His mom did sewing and ironing and cleaning to help with the family finances. After his father's death, after Billup moved out, she seemed to lose the will to go on and had died without anything in particular being wrong. One day she just didn't wake up. His folks hadn't gotten much of anywhere in their lives and they had such high hopes for him. And look at him now.

Billup knew he needed to stop drinking. He wanted his damn job in the police department. He was willing to go to the effing treatment program that Fowler mentioned. He wasn't really listening yesterday, but he'd call Fowler and get the name again tomorrow.

It had been one hell of a morning. Maybe the heaviest morning of his life. He had faced his devils, recognized they were of his own making, and was ready to make a change.

Tomorrow. But right now his head was killing him. He

had heard you could die if you stopped alcohol too abruptly. That's why they put people in a hospital to detox. It was life-threatening, and he wasn't going to run that risk today. Not now. Now that he was finally ready to square up and make a change. So, first? More medicine! He had been up for hours. He was ready to move. Celebrate his last day!

Janochek and the kids were standing at the edge of the lane beside the gravesite when Gates pulled up. He turned off the engine and got out, checking that he had put his phone on his belt.

"Hi," he said. "Thanks for waiting for me."

Gates introduced himself and noticed that Kiefer seemed to be growing uncomfortable. Gates thought perhaps Kiefer remembered his home visit, or maybe he sensed he was going to be interrogated.

"I'm here because I need to ask you all some questions about the Craddock gravesite and the Parker girl investigation."

Janochek seemed chagrined, Pearl seemed fascinated by this turn of events, and Gates would swear that Kiefer was about to bolt. Gates took a step closer to him so he could grab him if he moved.

"Mr. Janochek has told me that you believe the Parker girl may be buried in Craddock's grave."

Janochek was watching the kids as closely as Gates was. Pearl nodded. Murray was starting to perspire.

"Why, Pearl?" Gates asked.

"Murray saw somebody fooling with the grave," she said, "and the date's the same."

Gates had noticed that when he asked Pearl that question, Kiefer's eyes flashed over to her for a second.

"So, what did you see?" Gates asked, addressing Kiefer.

Kiefer licked his lips and looked away, then back to Gates.

"Um, somebody was digging around in the grave at night, I mean during the night after he was buried."

"You knew the day he was buried. How?"

"Uh, I saw it."

"Don't you go to school?"

"Yes."

"What time was he buried?" Gates asked Janochek.

"I believe just before noon, but I'd have to look to make sure," Janochek said.

"Are the records close?"

"Yes, right up there in the workshop." Janochek gestured toward the building up the hill sixty yards or so.

"Would you check them, please?"

Janochek left, and Gates turned back to Kiefer.

Kiefer was actually squirming, but Gates didn't think Kiefer was aware of it. Gates waited another minute or two to let the kid stew in his own juice. Then he made a deliberate show of getting his notebook and pen out of his pocket; turning to a fresh page; and putting the date, the time, and Murray's name at the top.

"That's *K-I-E-F-E-R*?" Gates asked, burning a hole through the boy with the intensity of his gaze.

Murray nodded, unable to meet the man's eyes.

"So." Gates was shaking his head, incredulous. "You saw them bury Craddock while you were nearly a mile away, in school?" Gates was clearly losing his patience.

Kiefer was looking at the ground. He couldn't seem to make himself look at Gates.

"You're lying, and I want to know why!" Gates put a gruff tone in his voice.

175

Kiefer began to tremble. Then he was yelling, "I can't tell you!" Louder, "I can't tell you!" Losing it.

"You can't tell me because you killed her and put her there!" Gates was yelling, too.

Janochek came hurrying down the hill.

"For God's sake, Deputy, back off! These kids are not your criminals!" He stepped over to Kiefer and put his arm around his shoulder, maybe to still the shaking, or maybe to let him know he was not so alone and exposed.

Gates took a few seconds to settle himself.

"You're right. Sorry I got so intense there," he said, "but this Parker investigation has me . . . Okay, I apologize for yelling, but something is cockeyed about this story, and I am going to find out what is going on, even if all of us wind up at the sheriff's office." Gates made a point of looking at Kiefer.

"I will stand by you both, no matter what," Janochek added. "No matter what. But I also think there's something missing in what you are telling us. I expect you to tell the truth right now, before this goes any further."

Tears began tracking down Kiefer's cheeks. Neither Gates nor Janochek had expected that.

Pearl stepped up.

"Uh," she said, looking at her dad standing with Kiefer, and then at Kiefer, as if to reassure him. "Uh, Murray is kind of . . . what do you call it? Extra sensitive."

"You mean he is . . . he has extrasensory perception?" Janochek said, trying to think along with her, trying to make sense out of her remarks. "He told you he's psychic?"

"Yeah, maybe. I mean no, he didn't say anything like

that. Um, but I think that's what they call it," Pearl said.

Kiefer had stopped crying and was still, eyes closed. Listening? Gates wondered.

"He sometimes knows things. Out of the air. And he got a, uh, really strong feeling that a girl was buried in the same place as the Craddock guy."

Mother spare me! Gates thought. Thank God I didn't have Drum join me for this.

"Are you saying that you two concocted this story because Kiefer had a *feeling* that the Parker girl was secretly buried with Craddock? That you didn't actually *see* anything suspicious?" Gates was trying to keep his voice down. Kiefer still hadn't opened his eyes. Pearl was nodding.

"Damn it!" Gates said with more force than he intended. "You aren't babies. You have to know that this is not an area to muck around in!" He wanted to hit something, break something. Kids screwing around, *playing*, when so much was at stake!

Either that or Kiefer did it.

"This grave because of the date, right? That's how you put it together? A matching date and a feeling? Should we dig up everybody buried on October seventeenth in northern California? What were you thinking, damn it!" Gates was steaming, couldn't seem to calm down. Nikki Parker deserved better than this shit!

For a moment Gates had an image of his son. Kneeling in his football team picture, helmet on the field in front of him. Dead at seventeen. He deserved better, too.

By four-thirty Billup was ripped. When he got up to uri-
nate, he fell forward onto the cement picnic table. It took
him a few seconds to stand and keep his balance. Sometime
during the afternoon, he had gotten mad. Mad at life. Mad
at people. They had burned him nearly every time he made
contact with them. He went through the list of people he
hated, ending with the cemetery geek.

He remembered that day at Vera's. She was barely
dressed, getting ready to come across to avoid a bust when
little Freaky came out of his hole to protect his mother! It's
not like Billup was going to hurt her. He was just going to
give her a slam-bam-thank-you-ma'am and be on his way,
until the kid spoiled everything. Well, that little shit didn't
know who he was screwing with. Billup would teach him an
all-time life lesson right now. Give him something to take to
the bank in case he ever considered butting in again. Of
Billup's list, that goonie was probably the nearest and the
least able to cause him more trouble.

He looked around for a weapon, a tree limb or a piece of
rebar. He was going to get some satisfaction. Start by erasing
that stupid little zitbag. And then, maybe he'd go teach the
mother a lesson about the cost of turning a person down.
Two-bit slut. Get his rocks off one last time before the damn
drug prison.

He lurched toward his truck and had a moment of clarity.
If he drove when he could hardly walk, he might get busted.
Make things worse. He could walk to the cemetery from
here. As he stood beside his truck, he had another thought.

He had a weapon! His dad's old .32 automatic under the seat of his pickup. There was a minute of indecision. Shoot the little shit or beat him to death? Maybe a little of both! People were going to pay. That much Billup knew.

Billup saw he had to climb a brushy hillside to reach the cemetery. He put the gun in his waistband and used shrubs and small trees to help him clamber up a game trail. When he got to the cemetery border, he crawled under the fence, took the gun out, and walked down toward the area where he had seen the kid before.

He stumbled on the blacktop but caught himself before he hit the ground. He straightened up carefully and continued at a slower pace, making himself focus on his balance. The more purposefully he walked, the better he managed it.

Down past the workshop, he could hear voices. He slowed even more and moved to the tree line beside the road. Maybe a quarter mile from the city street in front, he saw the kid. But there were people with him, standing around a grave. Talking. The geek, plus the caretaker and his daughter and a tall guy. *What the hell?*

The tall guy was standing facing a marker. Billup watched as the man sat on his heels to examine the stone more closely and then grabbed hold of the marker with both hands.

"Get away from there!" Billup didn't mean that. He had meant to say get away from the kid.

He was running at them with the pistol out in front of him.

Gates had his back to the gunshot. He turned to see a man running toward them with a pistol. The man slid to a stop about forty feet away, the pistol wavering in his hand but still pointed in their direction. Gates let go of the gravestone and fumbled at his waist for his gun. The holster was buttoned.

The man steadied the gun with his other hand and sighted down the barrel. "Don't!" he was yelling. "Don't move!" Everybody froze.

Though no longer advancing, the man was weaving slightly as he stood holding the pistol. When Gates put up his hands, away from his own gun belt, he reminded himself to be extra careful. He thought the man looked loaded, maybe high on meth.

"Okay," he said. "Take it easy. We're not moving. You win." Beside him, he heard Pearl gasp.

"Murray!"

"Don't move!" the man screamed again.

Gates looked where the Kiefer kid had been standing and saw him, instead, on the ground right at his feet. The boy was holding the side of his abdomen as if he could stop the blood from spilling down into the grass.

The man with the pistol took a lurching step forward, then turned and ran back up the hill toward the workshop.

Pearl rushed to Murray's side. "Help him! Help him!" she was yelling.

Gates tore the cell phone off his belt and pitched it to Janochek. He directed Pearl to put some pressure on Murray's wound and see if she could slow the bleeding. He told Janochek to get 911 and call for backup and medical support. Then he took off after the shooter, unbuttoning his holster and pulling out his revolver as he sprinted up the road.

He slowed as he got to the workshop area. He followed trees for cover until he reached the side of the building, and there he examined the door. No sign of forced entry. The door was closed and the screen was undamaged. Gates thought he would have heard the screen slam if the man had run inside. Besides, he didn't think the guy would want to be trapped. Gates figured he was chasing a stoner who was operating on pure instinct. He couldn't hear footsteps, but he guessed the guy was probably still running away full speed, heading either for the big parking lots by the rodeo arena or due south to Bluff Street and the Oakwood neighborhood.

Since the guy had a gun, he probably had a car, too. Gates gambled on the parking lots surrounding the rodeo grounds and that wooded picnic area along the river, down to the new Cascade Museum. He thought the guy could be a stock handler from one of those temporary mobiles behind the stables.

Gates ran carefully, gun ready. Two or three hundred yards up the blacktop, close to the top of the hill, he heard the man yelp and swear. Must have fallen, Gates thought, picking up his pace. As he crested the rise, Gates saw one of those burial buildings you could put a family in, some tall old-fashioned tombstones, and, behind them, a barbed-wire fence. When he reached the highest spot, where the road turned away to the north, he saw a piece of cloth waving from the top strand of a section of wire. Looked like the guy had torn his shirt in his haste to climb through. Gates jogged up to the cloth, put his hands on the wire, and leaned over to look down the slope.

"Freeze!" came from behind him, back near the crypt. "Drop your gun!"

Gates let his revolver fall from his hand. It hit the wire and bounced on the other side of the fence. *Shit!*

"Don't turn around!"

"Easy. Easy now," Gates said, still facing the slope. "I'm unarmed but there are cops on the way, so you better get out of here."

"Stop chasin' me!" the man slurred.

Gates could hear him moving steadily closer.

"Give me the gun!"

"I can't," Gates said. "It fell over the fence."

"Lie down!" The man was only a few feet away now.

"Don't do anything," Gates told the man, getting down on his stomach, facing the fence. "I'm not gonna move. I can't even identify you. Get out while you can!"

"You bastard!" the guy said.

Gates could feel the man practically standing over him. He wondered if he should make a move and try to take the man down. He wondered if the man was starting to pull the trigger.

Whunk!

Gates heard the thud of metal hitting bone and rolled away to see Janochek following through on a full baseball swing with a shovel. The man was falling forward, blood pouring out of the right side of his head. And then Janochek was diving on the guy, pinning his arms to his sides.

As he hit the ground, the man squeezed the trigger again and screamed as blood flew out of his knee. Gates was rolling back to help trap the gun. Everybody was yelling, until Janochek finished the man's fall by burying his shoulder in the man's spine and knocking the breath out of him. Gates got ahold of the gun and it went off one last time before Gates forced it out of the man's hand. For a moment, everything got still.

Gates reached for his handcuffs, and worried as he did that Janochek might have been hit. He got to his knees, aware of the metallic scent of blood mixed with liquor fumes. He got the cuffs on the man, who had stopped struggling and was making *eep*ing sounds, trying to get some air back in his lungs.

When the cuffs were tightened, Janochek pushed himself up and immediately retrieved his shovel. He was breathing hard and his eyes were wild.

"Don't you . . ." His shoulders were heaving. "Don't you ever shoot at my kids! Bring a gun into my cemetery!" Janochek was spitting as he threw the words at the man on the ground.

Gates stood and added his hand to the shovel handle, in case Janochek needed the extra willpower to keep from caving the man's head in. Gates and Janochek looked at each other for a minute and then Gates released the handle and went to retrieve his gun. Below, he could hear doors slamming, which probably meant backup had arrived.

Murray woke up in a pale green room on a narrow bed. A person, an older woman, was standing beside him talking to someone else. . . . His mother! He was foggy, but he could see she had on one of her thin dresses that showed her underwear. She was talking nonstop, and the older woman seemed to be trying to get a word in, trying to slow her down. He couldn't follow their talk, except that the older woman was like a broken record: "You can't be in here. This is pre-op. You can't be—"

Murray tuned them out. He was thinking about what Pearl had said back at the cemetery. She was wrong. He did not have pre-sensitivity or whatever she called it. He was crazy, pure and simple.

And then somebody else came in and they wheeled him away.

Billup had been taken by separate ambulance to the same hospital and admitted for surgery to reattach his ear and reconstruct his knee. He would be under guard, with additional suicide precautions, until he could be transferred to a clinical holding cell at the jail. Who knew what he would do when he sobered up and realized what had happened?

Back at the cemetery, Gates had read the man his rights. He asked him who he was, what he had been doing in the cemetery, and why he had attacked them. Gates got nothing but swearing in return.

At the hospital, after staff stopped Billup's bleeding and

before the surgeon arrived, Gates was present when Drummond identified the man as Billup and began interrogating him about the Parker girl. Billup was still drunk. He seemed surprised, even confused by the inquiry. He refused to answer any questions at all and asked for a lawyer.

The cemetery had been too chaotic to have a clear talk after Drummond arrived for the mop-up. Gates caught him in the emergency room after the interrogation, after Kiefer had gone into surgery. As far as Drummond was concerned, Billup was their new prime suspect for Parker, but the police didn't have enough evidence to indict. Right now, they didn't need to, because Billup was up on attempted murder, assault with a deadly weapon, and a host of other charges. Along with the current charges, the possibility that he might be a flight risk and a suicide risk would keep him in jail, probably without bail, for the next few days, if not months.

Drummond was frustrated about the motor-pool Ford. His partner had found out that the car had undergone three maintenance washings and vacuumings in the six weeks since the disappearance, and the preliminary examination they had just finished turned up nothing. He sent the car to the Department of Justice crime lab at the college.

Together, sitting in uncomfortable plastic chairs, Drummond asked Gates what he had been doing in the cemetery in the first place.

"Kids. False lead, I thought," Gates said, "but now I'm not sure."

On his way out, Drummond assured Gates that they would get this guy. "Crime lab will come through," Drummond said. "We'll buttress up your eyewitness, and that asshole will plea-bargain the body location to stay away from death row. Just a matter of time."

Gates wasn't so sure. If he himself had done it, he would stonewall till hell froze. It would be very, very difficult to get a conviction without the body. Reasonable doubt: Nikki Parker might have run off and could still be alive.

He shook hands with Drummond and went to the cafeteria to look for coffee while the policeman went to the station to start on the written report. Gates would leave the hospital as soon as Kiefer was out of surgery if, and only if, the kid was going to be okay. He felt honor-bound to sit vigil for someone who had taken a bullet that he thought was meant for him.

When Kiefer's doctor gave him the thumbs-up, sometime around dawn, Gates dragged out to the parking lot and got in his pickup. On the drive home, he made a plan to see Robert tomorrow. He would tell him the guy in the car that he remembered seeing was now in jail, and he would renew his offer of a sundae. Bruce, too, if he wanted to come along.

Murray woke up again some time later. He was in bed in a room that was pretty dark, except for some small colored lights around him. Monitors. Someone was talking. He felt like he was underwater. He tuned it in the best he could. His mother. She was still motormouthing to somebody he couldn't see.

". . . and then when I went to hear his Tuesday morning service, he was standing in the vestibule holding hands with that frizzy skank, Linda what's-her-name, and acting all lovey-dovey, and so that's when I said, 'Frank Walton, you can kiss my ass. . . .'"

Murray tuned her out and slid away to think about Blessed and how she used to sneak food she didn't like from her dinner plate to her pockets so her dad would think she had eaten it all and let her leave the table. Sometimes she'd forget she'd done it, she told Murray, and her room would start stinking. And she'd have to figure out something else to cover that up. She reminded Murray a little of Pearl. Funny, clever, tough.

The next time he woke up, as far as he could tell, it was day, and the sky outside his window was gray. He could see rain streaking the glass. He turned his head.

Janochek was sitting in an armchair on the other side of the tray table, near the foot of his bed; Pearl was in another chair, reading a book. Murray meant to say hi, but some garbled sound came out and both of them looked up.

"Mr. Kiefer may have rejoined the living," Janochek said, smiling and approaching the bed.

"Well, if it isn't old Wounded-in-Action." Pearl was standing, too. "I hate to admit it," she said, "but I was actually worried about you."

Murray tried to smile, but he stopped because his lips cracked.

"Don't try to talk," Janochek said. "We'll talk to you. But first let me get a nurse and tell her that you're awake and apparently alert."

He left the room and Pearl stepped closer to Murray's bed until she was against it. He wished she would hold his hand.

Her dad came back with a nurse in a white uniform,

who politely asked them to leave for a minute so she could talk to the patient and assist him. When they left, she turned down the covers and inspected a plastic tube.

"Is your catheter bothering you?"

Murray didn't know what it was, so he guessed it wasn't. He moved his head, no.

"Can you speak?"

He croaked a yes.

"Do you remember being shot?" she asked, covering him up and touching him lightly on the shoulder as she looked into his eyes.

He nodded.

"The bullet entered your side and went out your back. It doesn't seem to have hit anything vital, but we're going to keep you here and watch you closely for the next couple of days or so. It may have grazed your kidney.

"I don't want you trying to get up. Anything you need, and I mean *anything*, you push this button here on your rail and one of us will come." She showed him a small cigarette-lighter thing with a round light on the end. "Are we clear?"

"Clear."

She stopped at the door. "It may not feel like it at this moment," she said, "but you are very lucky."

CLAIRVOYANT?

The day after Kiefer regained full consciousness, Gates paid him a visit. Janochek was sitting in the vinyl armchair at the far side of Kiefer's bed. Janochek gestured toward the folding chair on the near side of the bed. Gates declined and approached the bedside.

"Son, I am sorry you were injured. I'm also sorry that I was so hard on you in the cemetery, but finding the Parker girl is real important to me and, most of all, to her family. I came here hoping you would tell me the truth about what's been going on at the cemetery."

The boy turned away from Gates and looked out the window. He appeared to want time to think. In the distance, an uneven line of haze topped the coastal range with scatters of thick clouds beyond, nearer the ocean. Gates got the sense that Kiefer was weighing the risk of his words.

"It was just a hunch," he said, turning back to face the law officer. "The date was such a coincidence and all."

Gates could feel the lack of connection with or trust from the boy. "What about what the girl said?" he asked, persisting.

"Pearl?"

Gates nodded. He could feel the boy being careful.

"Uh, we're kind of friends, spending a lot of time in the cemetery and all," Kiefer said.

Gates said nothing. Waited.

Finally the boy offered more. "She thinks I . . . she has a lot of faith in my hunches. More than I do, probably. She's only in ninth grade," he explained.

"Tell me about your hunches," Gates said.

The boy shifted his weight. Took another moment fiddling with the covers. "I sometimes try to imagine what the, uh, the person in the grave was like. Like how old they were when they died and what might have happened to them."

"I can understand that," Gates said, sitting down in the metal chair next to the bed. "I sometimes do that myself at graveyards."

"Cemeteries," Kiefer corrected.

"Cemeteries," Gates amended. "Have you ever been out to the beautiful one with all the colored paper decorations out by the Whiskeytown Dam?"

Kiefer shook his head.

"So what got you to thinking about the Parker girl and where she might be buried?"

"Everybody's been thinking about her."

"True," Gates agreed, evenly. "But most people don't have hunches about where she might be located."

"Well, I guess it's just natural for me, it being a cemetery and all, and then the date being the same."

"I suppose," Gates said, keeping his voice soft and his posture relaxed. "But again, not many people now, in December, can remember the exact day she disappeared without looking back in the paper. Most people would know middle of October, but not the seventeenth, for example."

This time the boy stayed silent.

Gates stood. "Mr. Kiefer, I realize you don't trust me. I can understand that. I don't imagine you or your family has ever had much use for policemen. I want to say one more thing and then I'm going to leave." He walked down to the foot of the boy's bed and stood facing him directly. "I don't want to harm or disturb you or your mother in any way. I am only, and I mean *only*, interested in finding the Parker girl and helping her family, because they're in a world of hurt." He paused to let that remark settle. "If, at some point, you feel you can help us with this investigation in any way, I would deeply and sincerely appreciate it." Gates gave a good-bye nod and turned to leave.

He was halted at the door by Kiefer's voice. "I felt like she was trying to get a message to me," Murray said, possibly addressing Gates but looking at Janochek.

Janochek leaned up in his chair but did not reach out to Murray or speak. Gates didn't turn around. Stood by the door.

"I felt like I could hear a girl crying. I didn't know who it was."

Gates heard a quick hitch in the boy's breathing and then what sounded like a long inhale.

Murray continued, "When I walked around the cemetery, the crying seemed to be coming from Craddock's grave. When I got close to it, I felt like she was telling me what had happened to her. Telling me she had been killed. Pearl guessed that she might be in there with Craddock."

Janochek bowed his head.

Gates still had not turned around. "So," he said, "have you ever had a hunch like that before?"

"No. Not exactly like that. No," Kiefer answered.

Gates turned then. "Did you know Nikki Parker?"

"I had probably seen her at school in a rally or something."

"Ever speak to her?" Gates asked.

Murray shook his head, no.

"Why did you think the girl you were sensing was Nikki Parker?"

"I don't know. I mean, I think I pictured . . . I don't know."

Janochek seemed like he wanted to break the tension. "Pearl may have figured that out. She led me to check Craddock's burial date," he said.

Gates had come back to the foot of the bed. "The part I don't understand, but that I'd really like to, is if you didn't actually know the Parker girl, how could you think she was trying to get a message to you that she was dead and buried in the cemetery?"

"I told you!" Murray realized he was almost yelling. "I told you. It was a hunch."

The more he listened, the more Gates felt the Kiefer kid might have killed her. One thing for certain, he was going to call Drummond and go for an exhumation order on Craddock. He considered reading the boy his rights but decided against it with Janochek there as a complicating presence.

Janochek stood. "What if the boy is clairvoyant?"

Gates whirled on him. "My God! Not you, too?"

Janochek held up his hands as if to shut off the diatribe. "*Murray* isn't claiming to be clairvoyant," he reminded Gates, his voice loud, probably carrying out into the hall. He took his volume down a notch but kept the intensity. "I'm asking you a civil question. You keep saying you want to get to the bottom of this, but you keep rejecting an obvious explanation. Surely you're aware that police all over the world have occasionally used psychics to assist with investigations."

"No wonder you work in a cemetery!"

Janochek seemed to get harder and taller. "Take that back," he said.

Gates hadn't realized how contemptuous he had become. His tone of voice. Good thing hospital rooms don't require a shovel. He took a breath to steady himself and apologized. "I'm sorry. That was inappropriate and uncalled for. This case seems to be bringing out the worst in me."

"No," Janochek said. "I know you're just trying your best to do a good job here, but I think you're letting personal prejudices close you off to some possibilities."

"So what do you think I'm missing?" Gates asked.

"Well, first, the obvious suspect is that lunatic who attacked us in the cemetery yesterday. Why was he so agitated and out of control? What was he doing there in the first place?"

"One of his favorite drinking places is just over the hill at the rodeo grounds," Gates said. "He was blitzed and came into the cemetery to raise hell. Drummond, the RPD investigator, says office buzz is the guy had something shady going with Kiefer's mom, and Kiefer interfered somehow. The guy, Billup, was out for revenge."

"Out for revenge in front of three other people? You're going to attack an idea like clairvoyance when you carry bullshit theories like that around in your hat?"

"Hey, the guy was crazy drunk! You expect him to make sense?"

"No, damn it, I expect you to," Janochek said. He looked around the room like he wished he could calm down a little more before he said anything else.

"All right," Gates said, wiping his forehead with his forearm. "Make your point."

"Do you know what clairvoyance is?" Janochek asked.

"No," Gates said, holding back his definition of new-age horseshit.

"Well, neither does anyone else," Janochek said. "It's a way of knowing that hasn't been explained, that's hard to study, that happens sometimes, and even the people who get the information don't really know how they know what they know."

"Great," Gates said. "And I'm supposed to do what with this data?"

"Just listen," Janochek said, "for a couple of minutes more."

Gates signified his willingness by lifting the annoyance from his face and giving the man his attention.

"First, you know extrasensory perception does occasionally occur. You've probably had premonitions or a sixth sense once or twice yourself, but this happens for some people more than others. What if Murray, here, really doesn't know exactly how he got this information about Nikki Parker? That may not make it any less valid. My daughter and Mr. Kiefer might not always lead with the factual truth, but they're not sociopaths, and they certainly didn't have anything to do with the Parker girl's disappearance.

"I'm willing to bet my entire life on that. Think about it. Murray says he's got hunches, use your own!"

Silence settled over the room as both men seemed to be considering. After a minute, Gates nodded to Janochek. "Okay. I'll take that idea seriously. But while I'm thinking

194

about it today, I need the answer to one more question. Where were each of you the afternoon and evening of October seventeenth?"

That question seemed to drop the temperature of the room by fifty degrees.

"Murray and I have nothing more to say to you, Deputy. If you have any more questions for us, you'll have to wait until our lawyer is present." Janochek turned his back on Gates and stared out the window.

It wasn't until after Gates left that Murray realized he had been practically holding his breath for the past ten minutes. His muscles were rigid and his side felt worse.

No one had ever stood up for him the way Janochek had just done. No one. Besides his mother's tinny pride about the idea that he would graduate from high school, no one had ever made an effort to understand and support him. He was feeling appreciated by a *living* person.

Murray noticed that Janochek was back in the armchair, reading a paperback. What about this clairvoyance stuff he had been telling Gates about? Was that what was happening? Murray really had no idea. He believed it was just the way he was wired. Honestly, he was glad. He actually loved Dearly and Blessed and Edwin. They were his friends, and he could count on them.

He put those thoughts aside when he remembered Gates's question. Did the Deputy really think he did it? Or that Janochek had something to do with it? He knew that all this confusion was his fault, his unwillingness to tell anybody but Pearl what he was doing. The last thing in the world that he wanted right now was for Janochek to be hurt because of him.

The next time Pearl visited, she called Murray "D.C."

"What's that mean?" Murray asked.

"Short for 'Direct Connection,'" Pearl explained, "because you're our hotline to Nikki. Perfect, huh? But other people will think it's about Washington or something."

"Hmm." Murray thought it over. He was touched. Earlier it was "Ol' Wounded-in-Action," now "D.C." He'd never had the kind of friend who'd give him a nickname.

"Okay, I guess," he said, "but only between us."

"Sure," she said. "So, can I ask you something?"

"Shoot," he said. She raised her eyebrows. They both laughed. "Not really," he said. "Yeah, go ahead."

Pearl scooted an inch or two closer, leaned forward, and rested both of her hands on his bedcovers. "What do you think is truly happening when you talk to dead people? Do you think they *really* talk back to you?"

Murray looked her in the eye. "Pearl, I swear to God, I don't know."

"Well . . . ," she said, but she didn't finish her thought. When Murray dozed off again, she was still beside him.

From the hospital, Gates drove directly to the Whiskeytown overlook. He walked through the visitors parking area to the bordering low stone wall, where he could sit and see the water below. Too cold. He went back to the car and got his coat and a blanket to sit on. There were no other cars. He was alone.

Rage. Impotent rage. For a moment, he thought about gambling, how some slots or some bets could smother his anger, give him a rush and he'd feel no pain. Never made things better, he remembered. He pushed the thought out of his mind.

He picked up his cell phone and called Mental Health. Told the operator that he was a sheriff's deputy and that he needed to speak with Peggy Duheen, briefly but immediately. She came on the line within the minute.

Gates told her about Kiefer. Could he be psychotic? Did she know of other people who had delusions about talking with dead people?

She said that was impossible to answer without a full psychological evaluation, and even those could be inconclusive. She said that sometimes adolescents have their first psychotic break in their teens, often in response to some increase in family stress or academic pressure. They usually become disorganized and uncommunicative. They have audio hallucinations or delusional ideas, grandiose or persecutory. In her experience, they usually fervently deny that anything is wrong with them, even after they've been admitted to a psychiatric hospital.

Gates thanked her profusely and let her get back to work. He made himself look closely at the water. Time to be still and gather his thoughts. The lake reflected the cloud cover, made it seem silver. He saw black silhouettes of birds in the distance, crows, he thought.

What Peggy had described didn't sound like what he knew of Kiefer. Gates felt worse than useless. In his frustration, was he starting to attack people who tried to help him? As a law officer, he would certainly need to completely eliminate Janochek and Kiefer as suspects, but he didn't think they were culpable. And, after talking to Peggy, he didn't think Kiefer was crazy.

He was mad at himself. Was he so close-minded that he had become blind? Maybe Janochek was right. Maybe the Kiefer kid was on to something. The burial date was a hell of a strong coincidence. Could he afford to dismiss it?

He had seen a couple of people who claimed to be psychic on talk shows or on late-night TV ads. They were slick. Charlatans. Those people couldn't be more different from the poor Kiefer kid. The boy was shy, scared, hell, scarred by his home life. The kid was a dweeb. But what if Kiefer really did see something and was afraid to tell him?

No stone unturned.

He was going to have to take this theory to Drummond. Tenacious, no-nonsense Drummond. Gates hated to bring up the idea of clairvoyance with him. If Gates was off-base, he would never get away from the teasing. Probably even a new nickname. "Night of the Living Gates." "X-file." "Poltergates." He cringed.

"Go."

"Drum, it's Gates."

"Yeah, well, nothing new out of Billup yet, but we're grinding on him."

"This is about something else."

"Another case?"

"No, the Parker girl. Uh, what do you know about clairvoyance?"

"What do you mean?" Drummond was starting to sound impatient.

"What if we got some useful information on the Parker girl's whereabouts from an extrasensory source?"

"Hey, Rome, I'm real busy here. Let me call you back."

"No, no, give me another minute. This could be important. What if the Kiefer kid is actually clairvoyant? What if he learned somehow where the Parker girl was buried? Wouldn't it be worth checking out? Haven't we always been willing to examine any detail that might be relevant? Kiefer thinks she's buried at Forest Grove. Couldn't we get an exhumation order based on that possibility?"

Gates didn't hear anything except the hiss of his cell phone. He wondered if Drummond had hung up.

"Gates, I tell you I'm seriously busy and you hold me up for this *Twilight Zone* bullshit? What is the matter with you? We got a suspect. We'll crack him and find the body. You don't need to go loco on this."

"Drum, what if we already know where she is?" Gates could feel sweat running down the inside of his shirt, wetting his collar, tickling his back. "Are you saying you're not willing to go to any lengths?"

More silence. "Drum, look, hey, the CIA has experimented with it. How crazy can it be?"

"If you think a question like that deserves an answer, you're around the bend."

"Drum, we go back a lot of years."

"Yeah, yeah, I know. Look, you want to write the request in *your* name from the sheriff's department, I'll ask Haggarty to take it to the judge, but I won't stump for it. You turn out to be right, you get the credit."

"All right. Thanks, Drum, but I don't want the credit. I want to nail the bastard."

"Yeah, me, too. Hey, I got to run. Talk to you later." Drummond broke the connection.

Gates couldn't sleep that night. Every time he asked himself what he knew for sure and certain about the Parker case, he felt sick. Everything was circumstantial: A shaky eyewitness with no lineup identification. A car that matched the eyewitness's description but was clean of any physical evidence. A suspect, a fellow law officer, for shit's sake, who denied everything. No body. No motive other than possible sex-related violence.

Had he even asked the right questions? Had Haggarty or anyone else combed the girl's high school acquaintance list for big-necked guys with big white sedans?

Maybe there was some coincidence that brought Nikki to her death. Billup driving past the gym at the very moment the pretty girl was walking out into the rain? But what if Billup was just an asshole and not a guilty asshole? Gates remembered the case conference at Mental Health.

What if Billup was in a blackout, in a lusty rage, and couldn't remember that he went after the girl and killed her? What if there was a wholly different situation in play? What else could have been going on that nobody had tipped to?

The following morning, shortly after he got to work, Gates called Haggarty and left a message asking him to run a DMV search on the high school students and staff who drove white sedans.

He got the next idea from Peggy Duheen. He called to thank her for her help yesterday and to offer a date soon for coffee or ice cream to show his gratitude. She asked him for news on the case, and he told her about the cemetery shooting; the troubling lack of hard evidence; and his lingering questions about motive, coincidences, and even the car.

"What car?" she asked.

"We think the suspect was driving a white American sedan with a whip antenna."

"Well, hell," she blurted, "I used to drive a white sedan with a whip antenna, so you might as well arrest me right now."

"I haven't widened my perp list to include women yet, but when I do, you're as good as jailed," he laughed. "You mean you drove one for the County?" he asked, curious about her remark.

"No, I meant that up in this heat, from Sacramento north, everybody and his dog has a white car," she said. "And whip antennas? My ex was into HAM radio and, when we were together, both our cars had whips. And there's citizens band and those new satellite radio things that have some kind of special antenna. I was just struck how looking for a car like that might produce a stadium full of suspects."

Gates missed her next few sentences while he was busy cursing himself. He was thinking that his assumptions might get an innocent person killed one of these days. He said a hasty good-bye and called Haggarty again. This time, he reached him in person.

"Hag, did anyone check citizens band or mobile HAM radio licenses? Don't you have to have one to operate those things in your car? Any male CB hobbyists or satellite radio buffs in Parker's high school crowd or in the campus neighborhood?"

"Crap on a post, is this Gates again?" Haggarty was harried and irritated. "Mr. Gates, I do not work for you. You already got me heading the DMV shitlist. They said one more request and I'll never drive again in California. Do the sheriffs have any investigators or any damn personnel that can actually use a computer? Do it yourself and call me when you know something." He hung up.

Gates was embarrassed. Haggarty was right. He called the high school and asked for a quick meeting with the principal and clerical staff in regard to the ongoing Parker investigation.

They met in the principal's office. "I'm following up on some information we've received regarding Nikki's disappearance, and I was hoping you all could help me narrow down a lead. Is there anything like a citizens band radio club or a satellite radio club here at school?"

The principal, a blunt-faced, fair-skinned man who seemed too young to hold that top administrative position, was shaking his head, no. A gray-haired man with large plastic glasses, possibly the vice principal, was rubbing his chin, thinking. The two women who were present started to speak at the same time. The younger one stopped; the older one continued.

"We have an Audiovisual Aids and Media club, but I don't think they have anything to do with the things that you mentioned."

The younger one piped in, "But Benny would know!"

"Benny?" Gates asked.

"He's what-do-you-call-it . . . uh, the school geek, or is it nerd?" The younger woman was uncomfortable saying those words, like maybe they were racial slurs.

"Electronics." The older man entered the conversation. "Benny has his HAM radio license and knows all about any type of electronic gear. He runs the sound for our assemblies, and everybody, students and teachers alike, uses him as a resource. If anyone would know, it would probably be him."

Benny turned out to be a handsome, smiling boy with neatly parted orange hair and a calm I-can-do-it attitude. "Hi, Mrs. Fender," he said, nodding to the older woman now behind the counter in the administrative office where Gates had been waiting.

She ushered them into a small counselor's room. "Let me know if you need anything else," she said, and left quietly, closing the door.

Gates introduced himself and then asked his questions about white cars and antennas. Benny looked away to his right and seemed to be scanning invisible memory files.

After a minute or so, he looked back at Gates.

"CB's not very cool, and HAM is real geeky. Walkie-talkies are the thing and they're cheaper than ever, sixty bucks or less at Costco, with a two- to five-mile range, and you don't need an antenna or anything.

"Twenty or so kids have satellite radio. It's pretty expensive still, so they're mostly the rich kids from the Sunset neighborhood. Those receivers don't really need much of an antenna, a stubby little wart of a thing, chrome or black usually, on the car roof in the middle at the back.

"I think I saw a whip on a white Civic, a sophomore guy in choir, he might be a HAM, and I think Gina has one on her white Infinity, but nobody I know has one on a Town Car or a Crown or a Caddy, that I've seen, anyway."

Gates waited while the boy looked away again.

"You know who used to have something like that?" Searching, searching . . . the boy's eyelids quivered; he was probing for the recollection. "What was his name? He graduated a couple of years ago, I think, and went to some-place like Chico or Sonoma. He played football. And he drove this big old white beast with an antenna on the back fender and some other stuff."

Benny turned back to Gates. "Uh, Crandall, or, or, Crallick. No, Craddock. Gary Craddock. I think that was his name. He was back here for his dad's funeral a while ago and I saw him around. I don't know if he had a CB or what. I didn't really know him. That's all I can think of." He opened his hands out in front of him and dropped them like a stage direction to indicate he'd done all he could do.

Gates managed to pull himself together long enough to

thank the boy for his help and then he was back in the office, asking Mrs. Fender if she had an address for a past year's student, a Gary Craddock. Inside he was whirling. Talk about a coincidence.

Mrs. Craddock was a dour middle-aged woman dressed in a stiff, shiny green dress that made Gates think of the word *taffeta*. Most people Gates knew would be in their comfortable after-work clothes getting ready to cook dinner. As she opened her front door, she frowned at Gates.

Gates introduced himself and, without further explanation, asked to speak with her son Gary.

"He's at college." She offered nothing else, not even a question about what he, a deputy, was doing at her home.

"He came back here for his father's funeral?"

"Yes."

"How long did he stay?"

"The day before the funeral to help with the arrangements, and he left the morning after. Is there anything else?"

"A few more questions. Would you rather talk inside, Mrs. Craddock?"

"This will do. What else?"

Gates was surprised by the woman's demeanor. He had not expected such a frosty reception, these terse responses. Most people in this area were somewhat ingratiating to a law officer on their doorstep, unless they were counterfeiting fifties in their kitchen or growing dope in their sunroom. He collected his thoughts and resumed asking.

"What kind of car does your son drive?"

A brief grimace. "He bought one of those dilapidated used highway patrol cars at an auction when he was in high school. I guess he and his friends thought that was funny." She clearly did not.

"And is that the car he continues to drive?"

"Yes, I suppose so. Has he had an accident?"

Gates thought her question came from fear of inconvenience rather than concern for her son's welfare.

"Does your tone of voice indicate that you're angry at your son?"

"That's a personal question, Officer. Do you have any further business here?"

Gates could see that something, perhaps a great many things, had not gone well for this woman. "I regret coming to you unannounced, Mrs. Craddock, but yes, I do have more questions. We can talk here on your porch, inside in the room of your choice, or downtown at the sheriff's department. Which would you prefer?" Gates kept his tone of voice even, but he hoped to underline his authority with this remark.

"Am I under arrest for anything?"

"No ma'am."

"Is my son?"

"No."

"Then ask your questions and leave." She had been holding the screen door open as they talked. Now she let it close and stood just behind it, arms folded, waiting.

"This arrangement will not be acceptable, Mrs. Craddock."

"I do not respond to threats, Deputy. I have recently lost a husband. I am in mourning and will not be harassed. If you have another question, ask it. If not, please be gone."

Gates stepped up close to the screen, where he could see her more clearly.

"How well did your son know Nikki Parker?"

There was no sharp intake of breath. Her arms stayed folded. But Gates wondered if he hadn't seen her shudder. As his eyes adjusted to the dim light behind her, he could pick up a dark living room where the drapes were closed, the lights were off, and the afternoon sun filtered around the base of the windows, creating just enough illumination to distinguish the vague shapes of furniture.

Mrs. Craddock's tone of voice was only slightly less exasperated now. "Diane Parker and I are cousins. That makes Nikki Parker and my son second cousins or cousins once removed or some such. They knew each other from family gatherings and, of course, went to the same high school. I wouldn't say they were friends. She never gave him the time of day, as far as I could see." She seemed to run out of words and energy with the last remark and stood still behind the screen.

When Gates had first met her, his grandmother's word *prissbutt* came to mind. Now he was thinking *enduring*. This woman in her expensive dress and empty house had been through something that had left her with this brittle anger, a scab grown over an injury.

"Did you see Nikki Parker the day of Mr. Craddock's funeral?" he asked her.

"No. I spent most of that day in my room, except for the services. Nikki didn't come to the funeral, that I remember."

"What about your son? What was he doing that day?"

"I saw him at the services. That's all. I don't know what he did the rest of the day. We didn't eat dinner together. I didn't want any company."

That remark struck Gates. This woman experienced her son as "company."

"Do you know what time he got home the night of the funeral?"

"No."

"Did he say anything to you that evening or the next morning?"

"No. I didn't see him after the service. He went back to school."

Gates took his eyes off her to locate his pen and pulled his notepad from his shirt pocket. "May I have the address and number where I can reach him?"

"If it's important, Officer, you can find that on your own," she said. "I have other things to do." She stepped back and closed the door.

Gates felt a moment of rage, felt the back of his neck heat up. *You're lucky to have a son.*

The annoyance fell away as he turned and walked back to his car. What would it have been like for Gary growing up in this family? Who would he turn to when his father died? Did he have an older brother or sister? He hated to ask Mrs. Parker, hated to reignite her anguish.

He used his cell to call Drummond.

"Go."

"Drum, Gates. When you started the Parker investigation, did you run into a family confidant or relative who was willing to help you with the family dynamics?"

"God, Rome, you do get around. Haggarty has been nominating you for lawman of the week all over the second floor."

"Drum, I have some new information, could be the break. Kid who graduated last year, cousin type of thing to Nikki, drives an auctioned highway patrol car. Gary Craddock. He's the son of the guy buried where Kiefer was shot. He was in town the day she went missing, the day of Craddock's funeral. She definitely would have gotten in a car with him.

"After the funeral, the day his dad died, kid had to be pretty upset. His mom is an ice cube. Maybe he was looking for comfort, got rejected, came apart."

"Gates, I'm thinking maybe you need a vacation, a little rest after the shooting thing with the kid. This *Oprah* shit has got to stop. You're making all these phone calls, got all these theories. We got a perp who fits! He's a goddamn maniac. He'll give it up. He'll cut a deal and it's over." His voice softened. "Rome, back off, give it some slack. This is a done deal."

Gates knew he better be careful. He did not want Drummond folding up their working relationship. Didn't want him to think he'd lost it. Drummond knew about his divorce, his kid's death, his gambling. He knew he was close to losing the man's respect.

"Drum, you're right. I do need to back off a little and take a breather. I've just been troubled by the lack of hard evidence. Nobody picked Billup out of a lineup, and all the rest of the loose ends. I'm trying to eliminate possibilities that will hurt us in court, that's all. Don't worry about it. I'll talk to you later."

Drummond hung up before Gates had finished speaking.

Gates drove back to his office, pulled his copy of the case file, and started reading. Half an hour into it, he had the name of the family member who had supplied most of the personal background information. Diane Parker had an older sister she had remained close to, who continued to live and work in Riverton. Marsha Virdon. Gates had heard the name and knew she was a realtor. He called her office.

They met at the Red Lion Coffee Shop for lunch. She was a heavily made-up fifty- to sixty-year-old woman who moved with a confidence that suggested substantially more successes than failures.

Gates explained that, in continuing to pursue lines of possibility regarding Nikki's disappearance, he would like to know whatever she could tell him about the family relationship between Diana Parker and Gayle Craddock and their children Nikki and Gary.

Over mixed-seafood fettuccini, Marsha talked while he wrote. She said that Nikki's family had always seemed pretty healthy to her—"I mean, Diana's still married to David and I know she loves him. Nikki's a bit of a twit, but show me a pretty high school cheerleader who isn't!

"Gayle Craddock's family, on the other hand, seemed troubled. The longer they were married, the colder Gayle became, but she never talked about it when we were all together, at least not to me."

Marsha told Gates that, for some reason, Gary had always seemed intense and changeable, "real up or real down," and that she thought he had a mean streak, but she wasn't positive about it.

"I heard that Gary was something of a partier and a bully in high school, but he was always polite at our get-togethers. I know you asked about Gary, but the thing I thought was interesting was that the daughter didn't come back from college for the funeral. She could have. She was just down in Long Beach, and she has her own car. Made me think she hated her father . . . or her mother. Or both."

The third day of Murray's stay, his nurse was excited about his progress and said she expected him to be discharged. She told him she had been unable to contact his mother and asked if he had any other relatives in town.

Murray remembered his mother had been cranking the day he was shot. He hadn't seen her since. Sometimes she went on a run that lasted several days and got pretty crazy. She was capable of picking up anyone or doing anything. He recalled some of the fights and some of the sex he had witnessed. If she was coming down from a spree, she might have taken some pills and could be out cold for a day or so. He didn't want to face that right now.

"Uh," Murray said, "just her brother, Mr. Janochek, my uncle. He'll pick me up if you give him a call."

"I thought the chart said he was a friend of the family," his nurse said, her expression slightly puzzled as she tried to remember what she had read.

"Oh, he is. He is." Murray felt a surge of energy, wanting to convince the woman of his lie. "He's been a very good friend of the family. It's just that, as her older brother, he hasn't approved of Mom's, uh, dating habits, and so I guess she doesn't claim him as a brother, but he'd be happy to take me home."

The woman seemed skeptical. "Well, we'll see what your social worker says when she comes in."

As soon as the nurse left, Murray found the phone book in the metal cabinet beside his bed and located Janochek's number. He got Pearl and quickly told her the situation.

When Pearl walked in, she was wearing a yellow dress. That was a first, as far as Murray could remember.

"Hey, D.C.," she said, smiling and walking right up to him. "You made it!" She leaned over and gave him a light pound on the shoulder. Murray thought, It's like I'm one of her teammates.

"Dad has a funeral till noon and then he'll be right over. He tried to call your mom, but he couldn't reach her, so he left a message. If they let you out, we'll drive you by your house and try to get her to let you stay at our place for a couple of days."

Murray couldn't remember ever feeling so good.

She slid the heavy metal-armed chair to the side of his bed, sat down, and leaned toward him, putting her hand on his arm. "Plus," she said, "I can't wait to get you back over there so we can find out who killed Nikki!"

"How'll we find that out?" Murray asked.

Pearl had that look on her face. "We'll ask her," she said, as if explaining simplicities to an idiot.

We.

"I'll help you walk and we'll go back to the grave and you can ask Nikki who killed her, and we can call the sheriff guy and give him the scoop," she said, dropping her disdainful look and becoming more animated. Excited.

Murray did not want to touch that Craddock tombstone again and feel that girl's misery. "I don't want to. I can't face it right now."

"Hey, I know you're still recovering, D.C., but those

police guys are stalled out and they need our help. It's okay. We can do it tomorrow."

"Want anything?" she asked as she lifted the muffin off his breakfast tray and took a big bite.

Gates took a day off. He got a commuter flight out of Riverton to San Francisco and the next available plane to Long Beach. He rented a car and met the daughter, Denise, at the Long Beach State Student Union. He showed her his identification and explained that he was here out of personal concern, gathering information for an investigation involving Nikki Parker. He said that he had no authority in this county, but that he hoped she would be willing to talk with him.

Her eyes flared for a moment. "Get it over with then. I knew this was going to happen sooner or later, anyway. Did he do Nikki, too?"

Gates didn't react, except to reach for his notebook and pen. The girl was tall and slender like her mother. She had fancy wraparound sunglasses stuck in her hair and wore an expensive-looking fleece jacket in a coral color Gates had not seen before. And the girl was angry. Like her mother.

"Did *who* do Nikki?" he asked, keeping eye contact, voice dead level.

"Daddy."

Gates saw water in the corner of her eyes.

"No. She disappeared the day of his funeral."

That seemed to surprise her.

"Why? Would he be capable of such a thing?" he asked.

"Oh, for shit's sake, he did us for years." A tear rolled down. "And everybody in his office, too. He was a goat. Did you talk to Mother? Yeah, you probably did, and she didn't say shit, right? Right?"

Gates stayed silent.

"She never said shit. Not a word. Not the whole time, and I know she knew. She saw him on me once. And I heard her ask him to leave Gary alone, but he didn't. He didn't leave anybody alone. God! I was never so glad that anyone was dead!" Tears from both eyes now. "But he was already dead, so why come down here and ask me about Nikki? Did she commit suicide?"

Gates shook his head. "I don't think so."

"Then what are you doing here?"

Gates met her eyes. "I came to ask you about Gary. About his relationship with Nikki."

"About Gary? About Nikki? About Gary." She pushed her chair back. "Oh, God, no! Oh, hell, no! No way!" She was yelling and getting up. People nearby were coming over.

"You asshole! No way. Leave me alone! Get away from me!" She moved away from the table and headed out of the union, almost running.

Gates felt a powerful hand on his shoulder. He turned to see a massive young man with a buzz cut pressing on him.

Gates said, "Ease up. I'm a law officer."

The young man, number 77, according to the jersey he was wearing, said, "Show me."

Gates held out his identification and the ballplayer released him. "Shouldn't upset people like that," he said, and walked away.

Gates took out his cell phone, called the Butte County Sheriff's Department, identified himself, and asked them to pick up Gary Craddock, Chico State undergrad, for questioning. He said it was in regard to an ongoing murder/kidnapping investigation and requested that they not, under any circumstances, question Craddock themselves or release him until Gates himself arrived that evening to talk with the boy face-to-face.

Murray had spent the morning on the couch in the Janocheks' small living room. Janochek had made pancakes with frozen strawberries for breakfast and then left for work. Pearl sat near Murray during the morning, reading and making a visible effort to look patient. Around noon, she went to the kitchen and came back with a peanut butter sandwich and a glass of milk.

"After you eat, let's go," she said, bouncing with the energy of anticipation.

Murray forced down a couple of bites and stood up slowly. Pearl had gone to the front porch and came back carrying one of her dad's old ski poles.

"The cane makes you look sick. This makes you look like an injured ski bum. Much cooler."

Murray accepted the pole. Pearl held the door for him and followed as he hobbled down the incline to Craddock's grave.

The sky was overcast, but there was no wind and the air was fresh, not cold. Murray felt a little nauseated. He wished he had gone to Dearly or Blessed first and told them he was okay, and reestablished some comfort. So much had happened. It was hard to know what was the same and what wasn't.

He was winded when he reached the end of the lane. He stopped at the headstone and turned to find Pearl right beside him.

"Go ahead and sit down and I'll hold you," she said.

He eased down and sat cross-legged in front of the dark

stone. He took a deep breath to ready himself for touching it again. He felt her arm circle his back. And a thought rose to the surface. *Where is the crying I usually hear?*

He reached out and put his hands on the marker. Nothing. He took his hands away and put them back again. Still nothing! He was blank.

"What's the matter?" Pearl could sense his puzzlement.

"Uh, I may have to do this more by myself."

"What did I do?" Pearl asked, concerned.

"It's not you," Murray said, unsure how to explain. "It's me. I . . . uh, I guess it's like grounding works with electricity. Like a short circuit. Or maybe being shot and all, I have to concentrate extra hard or something. Um, just move over a couple of feet and I'll try it again, and if I yell or anything, get me. Okay?" He had turned to look at her.

He could see her feelings were hurt. Her eyes searched his face for a moment and then she levered herself farther away. "Here?" she asked.

"Yeah, that'd be great." They looked at each other. "Uh, ready?" he asked. Trying to make her feel included.

She nodded, and he turned back to the tombstone and put his hands on it. The dim electric hum filled his mind and he made contact.

When Gates entered the sheriff's department in Chico, he was told that there was an urgent message waiting from a man named Janochek in Riverton. A female deputy showed him to an empty office with a phone. Janochek picked up immediately.

"Deputy?"

"It's Gates."

"Pearl made Kiefer go down to the tombstone again. This afternoon."

Gates remained quiet.

"Are you interested, or am I wasting both of our time?" Janochek asked.

Gates could feel his stomach pitch. "What is it?"

Janochek was silent for a moment, as if deciding. "Nikki says her cousin Gary did it. Thought you might want to know." He hung up.

When Gates entered the interrogation room, a muscular young man in a button-down oxford shirt and khakis was sitting at the table, hands clasped, head down, as if waiting for a scolding. Neither spoke, but the boy turned and watched Gates closely as he shut the door and came to sit down on the other side of the battered gray table.

Gary Craddock looked like a football player, a linebacker or fullback. His forehead and chin were prominent, but his cheeks were full and rosy. His neck was short and thick. Gates made an effort to relax the scowl from his own features. As he did, he noticed the young man's chin quiver.

Gates said, "Nikki Parker," and the young man's face crumpled and a sound escaped. Gates waited while Craddock got ahold of himself.

Craddock began shaking his head back and forth. Every time he gathered breath to speak, a sob broke. Finally he managed to get past the catch in his breath. He put both hands on the table, bracing himself, and looked up at Gates.

"I didn't mean . . ."

At least that's what Gates thought he said, but the sobbing started again and couldn't be contained. Gates did not remember if he had ever seen a big guy like that so openly broken.

After a couple of minutes, the Craddock boy pulled himself together and asked for a lawyer. Gates told him that, as of right now, he simply wanted to ask some questions. Gates said that, of course, the boy had the right to have a lawyer present, but if he exercised that option, Gates would have to read him his rights and formally charge him with murder. More, that he, Craddock, would be looking at jail here in Butte County, probably without bail until the court sorted it out, and then he would be extradited to Sierra County, where he would remain in custody pending an arraignment hearing. He told Craddock that he might be able to avoid all that jail time if he would choose to talk informally this evening and answer a few questions.

Avoiding eye contact, the boy again asked for a lawyer.

Craddock began his brief stay in the Butte County Jail, awaiting extradition. That same evening, Gates impounded the white ex–highway patrol vehicle and obtained a warrant authorizing its search.

Murray was staying back at home most nights. His mother had once again cleaned up from the speed. Now she was drinking wine and dating a gaunt older man who had a plan to make "a bunch of money" selling pet health insurance.

Murray was back to making his regular cemetery rounds, without the help of the ski pole. Some nights he stayed in the guest room of the Janochek home.

Gates took Robert and Bruce to the downtown ice cream parlor for sundaes with extra hot fudge and big scoops of nuts and cherries. As they ate, Bruce was lobbying Robert to see another movie, called *Road Trip*. "You ought to see the babes," he was telling Robert.

The three of them decided that the following week, if it wasn't raining too hard, they would buy a chocolate cream pie at the specialty grocery store and take it to Whiskeytown Lake for a picnic.

"And donuts, too?" Robert wanted to know.

"Yes," Gates agreed. "Lots."

Gates had had Polaroid pictures taken of the back of Billup's head, the back of Gary Craddock's head, and the back of his own. He brought them out of his jacket pocket and showed them to Robert when they were finished with the ice cream.

"Do you recognize any of these as the guy you saw arguing with the girl in the car that day?" he asked.

Robert looked them over. "Those haircuts are stupid," he said.

223

Gates abandoned the idea that Mr. Robert Barry Compton could ever identify the killer out of a lineup.

The lab's examination of Billup's patrol car had come up inconclusive. No loose hair was found, and the few fibers that matched white material from the cheerleading outfit could possibly have been deposited in the car by other circumstances.

The examination of Craddock's car yielded fibers that matched the high school cheerleading uniform, plus hair on the seat back and in the passenger floor area that matched hair collected from the brush in Nikki Parker's bedroom. Gary Craddock was arraigned and the bail set at $500,000. His bail was made and he was released.

He had pleaded innocent, saying that he was distraught on the day of his father's funeral and had been driving around the Riverton area trying to deal with his grief all afternoon and into the evening of the seventeenth. He expressed regret at Nikki Parker's disappearance and said he had given her a ride the afternoon before the funeral, which is probably how the fibers and hair got in his car. That story could not be confirmed.

Gates, this time in concert with Drummond, asked for an exhumation order on the chance that there was anything to Kiefer's hunch about the Craddock burial plot, but the Craddock family's lawyer was fighting it for lack of reasonable grounds.

The stalemate continued. And continued . . . until Pearl took matters into her own hands. Murray and Pearl had argued. He hadn't been able to talk her out of it. What a way to celebrate New Year's!

"You're just going to let her stay there?" Pearl challenged. "If it was me, would I just be lying down there crying and rotting 'cause you're too scared to rescue me?"

She looked mad enough to hit him. Murray had no reply. Maybe he would dig for her, if it were Pearl. But maybe not.

"Nobody else is doing it!" Pearl's eyes were blazing. "Nobody'll listen!"

Friend to the Deceased.

Pearl stomped out of the workshop, slamming the door so hard the lights flickered.

Murray knew. *She's going to get a shovel.* "I'll help," he said, but there was no one to hear him. He followed her out.

ABOUT THE AUTHOR

Charlie Price says, "I was walking in an old cemetery by a river in Northern California and found myself reading the inscriptions on graves. Many children had perished around the turn of the last century in a flu epidemic. The parents had hired stone masons to carve more elaborate inscriptions than I expected to see. I kept imagining the people in the inscriptions.

"Two years later, I wrote a story about a boy who was alienated from school and home, and found a cemetery to be a comforting sanctuary. The more time he spent, the closer he felt to the dead. I combined that story with an event from my community that had troubled me for several years. Murray, Pearl, Janochek, Mr. Robert Barry Compton, Deputy Gates, and Officer Billup began to speak to me.

"I was raised in Colorado and Montana, and I lived in Italy, New York City, Oakland, and Mexico before settling in Northern California. After I graduated from Stanford in the early 1960's, I had a dual career in education and mental health. Working in a variety of schools and hospitals, I grew to deeply admire the courage of those who lived and worked with mental illness on a daily basis. I admired the young people I came to know—their triumphs, as well as the valiant way they dealt with hardships and failures.

"I am married to a lovely woman who has surpassed my dreams for the past thirty years. Moreover, I hereby attest and confirm that my daughter, Jessica Rose, is *always* right. Unfortunately, as she will be the first to tell you, I am not of sound mind."

Charlie Price, in addition to writing and working with therapeutic groups, is a trainer, an executive coach, and a consultant who conducts business workshops and troubleshoots for private and public agencies. He is an avid reader, a decent singer and guitar player, a pretty fair free-throw shooter, and a hopelessly addicted fly fisherman.